JOYCE STRANGER

Joyce Stranger was born in London
and lived in Kent until her marriage;
she took a B.Sc. in biology and
chemistry at London University and
started writing as a freelance
journalist. Many of her stories have
been broadcast.

Her main interest is natural history;
during caravan holidays in this
country, Eire and on the Continent,
she has studied the habits of many wild
creatures, including deer, foxes,
badgers, pine marten, seals and birds.

Among her best known books are
*The Running Foxes, Rex, Casey, Rusty,
Zara,* and *Chia, the Wildcat.*

Joyce Stranger now lives in Cheshire,
her husband works for I.C.I. and
they have three children, two boys
and a girl.

Also by Joyce Stranger

CHIA, THE WILDCAT
ZARA
THE RUNNING FOXES
RUSTY
CASEY
ONE FOR SORROW
BREED OF GIANTS
REX
A DOG CALLED GELERT
WALK A LONELY ROAD

and published by Corgi Books

Joyce Stranger

Lakeland Vet

CORGI BOOKS
A DIVISION OF TRANSWORLD PUBLISHERS LTD

LAKELAND VET

A CORGI BOOK 0 552 09462 5

Originally published in Great Britain
by Harvill Press Ltd.

PRINTING HISTORY
Harvill press edition published 1972
Corgi edition published 1974
Corgi edition reprinted 1975

This book is set in 9-10½ pt Intertype Plantin

Corgi Books are published by
Transworld Publishers Ltd.,
Cavendish House, 57–59 Uxbridge Road,
Ealing, London W.5.
Made and printed in the United States of America
by Arcata Graphics,
Buffalo, New York

This book is fiction. All places in it and all people
in it are imaginary and are not based on any living person.

To Anthony P. Freeman,
Colin G. Nelson and Mike Clarke

Acknowledgements

I would like to thank Superintendent Spencer
of the R.S.P.C.A. and my numerous
veterinary friends who helped me with
information about technical matters while
I was writing this book.

CHAPTER ONE

THERE was never enough time.

Dai Evans rolled down his sleeves, and walked to the window, aware of nothing but tiredness. Behind him, three newly spayed cats lay in their cages, and the room reeked of anaesthetic. A dog, its leg broken by a speeding car, stared up at him forlornly. The plaster that held the newly set bone was uncomfortable. It was a cocker spaniel, a gay little dog, now only aware of needling misery and an aching leg and a curious malaise that was new and totally unfamiliar. The anaesthetic had almost worn off.

Dai Evans lived with his family in a vast rambling grey stone house on the edge of the fells, not very far from Bruton-under-the-Water, the village that owed its name to the falls that dropped over Horton Pike.

Beyond the window Hortonmere showed blue under a sultry sky. It was hot for the time of year. Elliott, the black kitten with markings like a white bikini, played with a feather, while Tia, his mother, watched him indulgently. Tia was a sealpoint Siamese and very beautiful. Sim, the black cat also belonging to the family, brooded on the wall. Most people, and Elliott himself, thought that Sim was the kitten's father, but Sim was neutered. He was interested in a blackbird that was chattering from the safety of a thin branch at the top of the apple tree.

The trout were rising in the beck at the end of the garden. Dai saw the silver flash in the sun and thought of the cool translucent water, of the soft grassy bank, of the dipper that swayed on a branch above the inlet where he had fished, long ago, when he was young and time was endless and there was no urgency.

Urgency was the ringing telephone, with a message from a distant farm; urgency was a cow, ill after calving; urgency was a horse that had jumped a barbed wire fence and torn its belly;

urgency was a case of fowl pest, or of swine fever, or of foot and mouth. Urgency was a dog lying on the operating table, injured by a passing car. Urgency was a child crying when a well-loved pet was put to sleep. And not only the children cried.

It was an idiot life. It was a life filled from dawn to dawn, with night an interrupted interlude. It was an impossible life. It was an insane life. It was the only life for him.

One of the cats wailed. She was rousing from the anaesthetic. He walked over to the cage and watched her, conscious of a small stir of pity as she weaved her head from side to side, and tried to stand on legs that had no desire to obey her brain. She staggered to her feet, and fell, and tried again. It was a good sign. By next morning she would have forgotten everything. He looked at the other two cats. Both were coming round. They were all reacting normally. No trouble there. Dai was a very competent vet.

He went out into the passage. Susie, his youngest daughter, was racing towards him, shouting, while Elliott, the black kitten with the white bikini, came towards him full pelt, dragging the stuffed koala bear that was Susie's special toy. Dai fielded the kitten expertly, cradling him for a moment while he retrieved the bear. Susie snatched it from him, and ran off again.

'Children,' he thought, watching her speeding figure. She was a problem in her own small way. She could not bear any creature, large or small, to die, and when it did she treated her father to stony silence, ignoring him completely. He should have saved its life and he could have done if he had tried. She could never see any reason why death should win. Dai dreaded having to put a very old or sick animal down. Susie always took more than a week to forgive him, so that now she was shielded as much as possible from everything that went on. But that was far from easy in a village as small as Bruton-under-the-Water, where everyone knew everyone else and gossip was widespread, and adults forgot that children had ears.

There was an hour to spare before the next surgery. The fish were rising, and the sun was low on the horizon. A mist masked the far fells, and the trees were turning to gold. An hour beside the water would be relaxation. An hour's peace. An hour's respite. He turned back to the house to fetch his rod and was looking for the rest of his tackle when the telephone rang.

A cow was calving at Hollow Lane Farm, a little Jersey who always had difficulty. It was going to be a long job. Surgery would have to wait. He hoped there would be nothing else urgent. He must get a partner. It was impossible, coping single-handed.

A moment later he was on his way. Sheila Evans, finding the forgotten rod lying on the dining-room table, picked it up and put it away carefully. Poor Dai. He never did manage to go fishing. The trout were still jumping. She closed the window and went to look at the cats. Tomorrow was Saturday, but that meant nothing. One day was like another. Much too full. There were cats and dogs and horses to feed, and the family too, and the surgery must be cleaned, and as Dai had gone out, she would have to supervise the recovering patients.

If only there was a breathing space. If only she and Dai could escape for an evening alone, or climb the fells, and look down on the water. It was no use. She stooped to pick Elliott up, and he rubbed his small black face against her chin and mewed, and lifted his nose to her face and purred confidingly. There were times when she thought that four-legged creatures were infinitely preferable to the human race. His small warm furry body was brief comfort. She put him down again. There was so much to do.

If only there were more time.

CHAPTER TWO

MOLLIE, Dai's eldest daughter, walked into the kitchen, waving a small red flag that she had made from coloured paper and a knitting needle. Sheila stared at her daughter, whose days off were rare, as she worked at a stables which was always busiest at weekends, so that she was only free once a month.

'Oh, no!' Sheila said.

It was the last straw. It was Saturday and surgery was busier than usual. Every owner seemed to wait for the weekend before bringing in a sick animal. Dai had been out half the night with a calving cow, over at Steve Johns' farm. She herself had been up as well. Chloe, a beautiful pedigree Burmese queen belonging to the Wellans, insisted on having human company when she had her kittens, a trait that was profoundly irritating, but no one could convince Chloe of its inconvenience.

The last kitten arrived without complications as Dai came home. Sheila went down to the kitchen to make coffee, and they sat drinking it peaceably, enjoying a rare and uninterrupted conversation, while Chloe brought her kittens, proudly, to show the vet, and curled round them protectively. Tia came to inspect them, and Chloe spat at her, furious.

Dai removed the Burmese to his study. Chloe was wary of strangers, and unused to children. The study was sanctuary. There Dai kept the drugs that he needed, and his gun, locked safely in a high cupboard, and all his reference books, and his big desk and his record books. Chloe was safer there than anywhere else in the place. The children adored kittens, but there was always the danger, with highly sensitive animals, that they might, if disturbed, eat their litter, giving way to a misguided idea that this would keep them safe from interference.

The day continued as it had begun. There were three bills in the morning post, the first for a large sum due for repairs to the roof, the second, not much smaller, for the new run of kennels for dogs recovering from operations. Tim had broken the coffee-pot, and Susie had fallen over Deedee and cut her knee, just before Mollie had taken the family joke a step further and hoisted a storm warning.

'Now what's happened?' Sheila asked.

'He's had to put a cat to sleep because it had been neglected. I heard him telling the owner off. I'm glad it wasn't me!'

Mollie was petite and elegant, a smaller version of her mother, dark eyes and dark ponytail contrasting with a skin that was delicately tanned by the summer sun. She rarely wore anything but jodhpurs, having little money to spare for other clothes. She looked up at her mother, her expression worried. Dai was always 'he' and never Daddy to any of them when something had enraged him. And nothing upset him more than seeing an animal that had been brutally treated.

Tim, putting his head round the door, saw the flag and sighed deeply.

'All right,' Sheila said. 'Tell the others. Action stations!'

'It's no use telling Susie,' Tim said. 'She's howling her eyes out in the barn.'

'She probably saw your father take the cat to the incinerator,' Sheila said, exasperated.

Susie was liable to cry for hours if an animal had to be put down, even if it was not personally known to her. The child knew how she herself felt when one of her own pets died. Dai refused to allow his youngest child to keep any creature that was short lived. None of them could bear the storm of sorrow when the inevitable end occurred. They never let Susie see any kittens brought for Dai to destroy, as, if she saw them, they had to be kept, and found homes.

Mark, racing through the door, about to bang it, was dressed for football. Mark was the family problem, the third of the children. At eleven he was stocky, freckled and homely, until a vivid smile lent brilliance to his face, and splendour to brooding brown eyes that, uncomfortably, saw through adult hypocrisy and treated it with the contempt Mark thought it deserved.

Mark was responsible for bringing them Deedee, the family's Great Dane. He had been brought home with two black eyes and a bleeding nose by the village policeman, having attacked three village lads, all much older than he, who were tormenting the pup. He took it from them, and the family had a new pet. Deedee from then on devoted her life to protecting them from real and imaginary dangers with as much dedication as Dai brought to his practice.

Mark saw Mollie's flag and hastily changed his mind, closing the door gently and quietly, before removing his books, his satchel and his blazer from the kitchen window-seat.

Mollie had already taken practically everything that might cause annoyance and hidden it. Sheila put the kettle on for coffee, before going into the study to hide the bills under the desk jotter, while Chloe purred her pleasure from the corner. Perhaps the kittens would soothe her husband when he came in for his lunch-break and to read the morning mail.

There was a yell from the surgery.

'Sheila!'

She ran into the hall and met him at the door which led into the house.

'Some damn' fool woman's brought a dog with distemper here. It's been sick on the waiting-room floor. Clean up and use gallons of disinfectant. God help me, I'll do murder one of these days. I've sent the idiot home and told her I'll call. And remind me to get more vaccine. She's probably started an epidemic.'

He closed the door with such restraint that the gesture was more emphatic than a bang. Sheila fetched the bucket, and mop, and paper from the kitchen roll, and shut Deedee in the kitchen. Mollie had gone outside to clean out cages for her, and to pet Conker, her pony, who adored being fussed over.

Sheila sighed. It was no use wishing. She scrubbed the floor furiously. All they needed was a distemper epidemic to make life hell, and there were still four dogs waiting to see Dai. The vet had sent them and their owners to stand outside, where there was less risk of infection.

The children had gone. She looked round the room. All was tidy, and nothing seemed out of place. Dai would be in a towering rage when surgery finished.

The last patient trotted down the drive, his tail waving, Sheila identified him as the boxer from the bakery, having a course of three injections to cure an abscess caused by a fight. There would be a box of cakes sent up later in the day, by way of thanks, from Rascal's owner. The surgery door slammed with a vicious bang.

'Where the hell's my coffee?' Dai called angrily, erupting into the kitchen with such forcefulness that Deedee hastily crept outside, hoping to remain unnoticed, and Rusty, the fox, shot under the table. 'I'll have it in the study.'

He turned on his heel. Later that day Sheila would hear exactly what had upset him, but now was not the time to ask. Dai walked into the study. Sheila, checking it five minutes before, had not noticed Elliott. Elliott, now twelve weeks old, was more inquisitive than ever. His white bikini and his four white socks were in sharp contrast to his sleek black coat, and he kept them spotlessly clean, aided by Tia, whose adoration for her kittens was wearing thin. They were very exhausting, and though Sim helped her guard them from danger, neither of them could cope adequately with Elliott. Also she had just been spayed, and had not yet recovered completely from the operation. The stitches pulled and annoyed her.

Elliott had found a dead mouse. It was a very small dead mouse; a very dead, dead mouse that Sim had actually put out of existence two days before and forgotten. Elliott knew a little about mice. He knew the smell, and the excitement engendered in him by the idiotic tail that twitched and hung behind the creature, like a piece of twisting string. He could catch string, which Susie often dangled for him, but mousetail was different. Apart from its smell, it moved much faster, and he could never judge its position. When he jumped the mouse had gone, and sometimes he fell over, which hurt his dignity, especially if one of the children saw him and laughed.

This mouse was satisfying. He could carry it and pretend that he had caught it himself. He showed it to Tia, but she was busy stalking on her own account and took no notice of him. Sim was asleep on a rafter in the barn, basking in the sunshine. He was out of reach. Elliott could not miaow to Sim – who, he was certain, was his father – as if he did he would drop the mouse. He carried it down the drive. There was nobody there. Elliott prowled home again, the mouse still dangling from his jaws.

Sheila did not see him slip into the study behind her, and did not know that she had left him there when she closed the door. Elliott settled behind the big leather chair to play with his trophy. It was very heavy for a small kitten and tired his mouth. Furthermore, he had been awake for a remarkably long time, and he needed somewhere comfortable to sleep. He walked to the hearthrug and considered. The leather chair had been scored by generations of claw-sharpening cats. He could hook his claws into the arm, and he began to mountaineer, still carrying his mouse. It was a long hard climb for so young a creature. He sighed with content when he achieved the cushion, and curled up with his treasure under his paws.

Dai flung the door open and yelled to Sheila to hurry with his coffee. Even Elliott had lived long enough to know the storm signals. He rolled off the cushion and crept hastily under the chair and pretended he had never happened. Dai, walking to his favourite chair, longing to sit down, saw, in the middle of his cushion, a very dead mouse.

He picked it up by its tail and marched into the kitchen.

'The least you can do is keep the cats out of the study,' he shouted. 'Look at this. One of them's brought a dirty great rat into the house. It's time those beasts were kept outside. Out, every one of them. They can sleep in the barn. It's absurd to allow them into the house. And you needn't bother with coffee. It should have been ready. I can't trust anyone in this house to do a single thing properly.'

He dropped the mouse on the floor. Sheila hated mice, and above all, she hated dead mice. The back door slammed. An engine roared to life and the Land-Rover hurtled down the drive. Sheila gave a sigh of relief and busied herself by cleaning the waiting-room and surgery.

Dai, driving to the farm beyond Hortonmere, where Steve Johns bred dairy cattle and bacon pigs, pulled into the edge of the road and sat looking over the fells. The wide spaces were a benison. Autumn had come, spilling bounty. The ground was bright with fox-red bracken, the trees flaunting brilliant leaves; rosehips starred the hedges at the boundaries of Steve Johns' field. A muscle twitched at the edge of Dai's mouth, and he leaned forward to look under the dashboard, where he kept his hidden vice, safe from the children's greedy fingers. As he unwrapped the chocolate, he relaxed, and the anger died from his eyes.

He did not know what to do. The little cat he had been forced to destroy had been only ten months old, elegant, gentle, and affectionate. Her eyes had stared at him, desperate with fear, and when he picked her up he knew that she was starvation thin, and the infection that had hold of her was killing her, mercilessly. He examined her, finding signs of worms, and fleas, finding an abscess under the fur of her neck, which had eaten deep into her body, finding a cracked rib, and cuts and bruises all over her.

The girl who had brought her for treatment stared at him defiantly. The cat had been brutally used. It had been half starved and it had been kicked. He ought to notify the authorities, ought to find out chapter and verse, and he hated the thought. He thrust it from him. The cat was out of all pain. Susie had seen him take the lifeless body out of the surgery, and her sudden sobs had appalled him. He wished the child had not been there, but it was useless and Susie would have to learn. Nothing lived for ever.

Steve Johns was waiting. He was an especial crony of Dai's, a tall man whose shock of dark hair was turning to grey, matching bristling grey eyebrows that were more mobile than his lips; heavy folds of skin drooped over cheek and chin, and a love of good food revealed itself in a paunch and in plentiful flesh on arms and legs. Steve revelled in his life, and his farm was his sole love. His wife always said she came a poor hundredth in his esteem, after the farm and all the animals.

Both Dai and Sheila loved visiting Deep Willows. The farmhouse had been built when Elizabeth was queen and Drake pirated the Spanish Main. Its blocks of dressed stone stood strong against the gales, shielded by stands of tall trees from the wicked wind that hurled across the fells. The wind roared, whistled, and shrieked in the night, so that children were sure the house was haunted. Steve Johns had a kinship with his beasts. He had a way with all animals, and often Dai felt that the farmer knew far more than he from a practical angle. At times, his foreknowledge was uncanny.

Dai, leaning on the gate that led to the piggery, told Steve about the cat. Steve was definite. The owners must be made to realize their crime. Dai had no choice. They must be prevented from owning another animal. Dai nodded. He had known he had no choice, but he hated having to alert the authorities. He wished that people would learn humanity. Too many who walked on two legs were far from human beings.

The two men stood talking. The farm was rich and well managed. The cattle were wintered in, but in summer taken to roomy paddocks where they could graze in comfort. The milking parlour was new and modern, and Steve Johns' cattle manager was also dedicated, so that often at night he had to be sent home, because he had stayed overtime to see that a calf that had been refusing food was feeding again, or that the nightman was well briefed about the cow that was to calve in the next few hours.

'I want you to look at Jubilee,' Steve Johns said. 'She caught her foot on the edge of a spade yesterday. Looks infected. And Charity's due to calve tomorrow. I think the calf's every whichway. So you'll be needed.'

Dai dressed the cut leg and gave the cow an injection, and went to look at Charity, who had long ago been hand reared and who preferred people to cows. She rubbed her velvety muzzle along Dai's cheek, and he humoured her, and stroked her neck and spoke to her as he felt the lie of the calf. Steve was right. Dai hoped she'd calve by day. Too many nights had been broken recently and his temper was suffering. He should never have shouted at Sheila. He felt mean about it. He must try and remember to take her some small gift on his way home. He never did remember.

Lysbeth Johns called him, and he joined her over a cup of coffee in the big kitchen, where rosettes decorated the dresser, and rows of Toby jugs laughed from the shelves. A sheepdog bitch lay under the table, nursing four pups, and Dai went to admire them. Their eyes had opened the day before. The bitch knew him and licked his hand and groaned a welcome, delighted to be noticed. The pups were well bred, and would be trained and sold for a sum that, to a shepherd, was a small fortune.

Dai was too aware of work to do, as they drank their coffee, and talked briefly of the weather and the harvest, of prices of beef and lamb and pork, of Charity and her calf, of Dai's children, who always called on Lysbeth when they were near.

Shadows darkened the sky, as bleak clouds gathered over Hortonmere, promising rain to come. The valley flooded easily. Too easily. Dai glanced up before walking to his Land-Rover, and saw the postman hand a letter to Steve. The farmer frowned as he opened and read it. Dai called to say that he was going, but Steve did not hear him. He stood, staring at the paper in his hand, looking up absently when his wife spoke to him, and nodding briefly, before re-reading the typed words. Dai hesitated, wondering if his friend had had bad news, but it was none of his business, and he did not care to ask. He drove away, irritation niggling. He would be late for lunch and he hated spoiled food, and it was almost time for the next surgery. The animals would have to wait.

He accelerated, feeling old, and tired, and overworked, and unduly worried by the look he had seen on Steve's face. The farmer might have received a death sentence.

The autumn brilliance was shadowed as he drove home. His thoughts ranged freely. The road was empty, except for an old car driven by a local farmer, who waved as he passed. The sky clouded to grey, promising rain before nightfall. If only he could help his friends more. Some men were so alone, so defenceless and sometimes, suffered so much, while others went their blithe way, regardless.

The man who strode into the road startled him. He swore and braked.

'I damn' near killed you,' Dai said furiously.

The man was Brook Holler, and where Brook was, trouble walked often. Dai had found two dying dogs in appalling condition on Brook's slipshod farm, and had him prosecuted and prevented from keeping dogs since. Brook owed him a grudge, and if Brook owed a grudge he paid it. Two farmers had lost good collies, supposed to have been trespassing on Brook's land. The bodies were there, tell-tale, among Brook's sheep, yet neither dog had ever been known to wander.

'Your damned fox is killing my sheep,' Brook said.

'Don't be daft, man.'

Dai rarely minced words with those he disliked. Tact had never been his strong point, and Sheila worried lest one day his tongue got him into real trouble.

17

'My fox never wanders. He's in the house all day, and all night, and only let out into the paddock. He can't get out.'

'I warned you,' Brook said. 'I see him again and I shoot him.'

'If there's a fox among your sheep you're welcome to shoot it. It's a wild one, and not mine,' Dai said.

'I see your fox outside the gates of the House of Beasts just once, and I shoot it,' Brook repeated. He glared, and eased his gun, and marched off, a big surly man, more often drunk than sober, and no man to have as an enemy.

Rain lashed across the windscreen. The summer fells, a blaze of heather massing from one lake to another, were constant pleasure, but when rain arrived from the sky, and grey clouds shivered over the land, they were miserable places and Dai wished he did not have to spend so much time in his Land-Rover driving from farm to farm. Rain, too, was an added penance, as the lanes were muddy, and the fields morasses through which he ploughed ankle deep to mud-coated beasts that shivered, soaked to the skin.

There was, too, too much time for thought. The worry about Rusty was a new one, that had not occurred to him before. He did not like keeping wild beasts as pets. It was unfair to them. In the summer, there were campers of all kinds, many reasonable folk, but others were youths escaping surveillance, carrying an airgun, shooting at anything that walked on four legs or ran, or flew. They went at the end of the summer, but Brook was always there, a constant threat to his peace of mind. He reached home and braked savagely.

The children crept away from him, seeing his frown. He ate without tasting his food, failed to hear Sheila's queries, and, as he went into the surgery, eyed the telephone, wondering if he should phone Deep Willows and find out if all was well. He dismissed the idea, and began the afternoon by giving a Siamese kitten a routine preventive inoculation against enteritis. The task lightened his thoughts.

The kitten was healthy, lively, and delightful, and greeted him with pleasure and a throbbing purr that was only slightly dimmed by the stabbing needle. The prick was soon forgotten, and Dai gave the proud new owner a diet sheet, and instructions on times of feeding, and watched as the little cat was lifted gently and carried out to the waiting car. The kitten reminded him of Elliott, and now, as he thought of the mouse left on his chair, he was able to smile, and the memory of Steve Johns receded, until it was no more than an unresolved nagging query in the background of his mind.

CHAPTER THREE

THE Swan was busier than it had been for weeks and Mrs. Jones bustled around with brimming glasses, while the Huntsman worked overtime at the bar. He had been her lodger and barman now for several years, and eased her burden considerably. He was a little, dried up, stick of a man whose small body seemed to be shrinking more than ever, but he was able to do enough work in a day to put a younger man to shame.

Times were changing in the village, but the Black Swan had not changed with them. The big kitchen, with the long scrubbed table, was still more popular than the small formal rooms where visitors sat uncomfortably on shiny leather chairs and sipped gins and tonics and dry Martinis.

In the kitchen, everyone drank beer. Even the dogs drank beer, and waited for the drips that fell from the table, and eyed each other warily, but did not dare fight. Steve Johns had come in early, and Mrs. Jones was uneasy. He was usually a temperate man, but tonight a devil must be gnawing him, for this was his fifth double whisky, and he with a car outside.

She was relieved when Dai arrived on one of his rare visits. She walked across the room to speak to the vet, and to ask him to make sure that Steve did not drive himself home tonight. There was only one way to do that and Dai went out again into a night lit by a thin new moon, with rain promised before daybreak, and removed the distributor cap, and took out the rotor arm from his friend's car. He himself had only dropped by on the off-chance, as his worry about the farmer would not be stilled. He was glad he had come, but when asked what he would drink, he settled for tomato juice. He expected a mare to foal that night and Steve's own cow, Charity, might calve early, and he anticipated trouble.

Steve had retreated into a nightmare world of his own. He glared at Dai, almost without recognition. Dai took his tomato juice, exchanged a swift, anxious, and informative glance with the Huntsman, and sat down beside his friend. He wanted to ask questions, but did not know how to start.

He sat, waiting. Steve Johns drained his glass, and held it out for a refill, but Mrs. Jones had given the Huntsman a curt nod of refusal and, deliberately, nobody noticed. The background of talk continued and many questioning glances crossed the room. The farmer was usually the centre of a laughing, teasing group, quick with witty retorts, and full of jokes. His sour face damped everyone's pleasure.

'We'll have some coffee, Mrs. Jones,' Dai said, as the landlady passed him on the way to the sink. She had anticipated his request and brought a tray which had been ready laid. The big two gallon copper kettle, that sat above the open fire, on a trivet, was always on the boil. Dai poured out, and passed a cup to Steve, who took it as if he had never seen such a thing before. The coffee restored some life to his face. He looked at Dai and his big mouth twisted wryly.

'God rot all politicians,' he said unexpectedly, and viciously, and handed Dai the letter he had received that morning. Dai read it twice before its meaning was clear and then he too exploded.

'They can't,' he said, furious. 'They bloody well can't.'

The seated men stared at him.

'As far as I can see they bloody well can.' Steve looked gloomily at the men in the room.

'They're going to flood the valley,' he said. 'It floods so easily, they reckon it would be a good idea to keep it that way, and extend Hortonmere. The cities need more water. Deep Willows will be drowned. There will be others hearing soon. And where in God's name do we go?'

For one appalled moment nobody answered. If the valley were flooded then Deep Willows would be deep indeed; and others would go with it: Bess Logan's cottage and Joe Needler's place and Josh Johnson's land, where his Shire horses grazed, would all vanish. Josh had had a bad spell, but he was well and truly on his feet now, and the edict would come as a severe blow. And the Wellans' farm, Sheerlings, would also disappear under the water.

'My family's lived there since the house was built,' Steve

Johns said heavily. 'There's always been Johns at Deep Willows. And where would we go? I've got no sons, but we've left the farm to my brother's boy, Adam. Adam's thought of it as his almost from the time he could talk. He's almost finished at Agricultural College now, and has a job lined up waiting, to get some outside experience, and after three years was coming in with me as partner. He's a Johns too. I promised my brother. Farming's born in the lad and Deep Willows has always been his second home. I've been working for that for twenty years. It's not bloody well fair, and that's putting it mild. Bloody bureaucrats. What do they care?'

The ringing phone interrupted him, and Mrs. Jones answered it, almost thankful for the call that had put a temporary end to the conversation. She had no comfort to offer, and was shocked to find anger riding her so hard that she was trembling. If Steve Johns could be turned out of his home, no one was safe, and which of them would be the next? And though the Swan was on high ground, too many houses lay in the valley and what would happen to business then, with so many gone? And where would they go? They all belonged here and had belonged all their lives. Behind her, the men sat silent, grim-faced, each one worrying about his home, working out whether it lay high or low, and what might happen.

Ned Foley eased stiff legs and scratched his grey shock of hair, emptying his glass. He picked up Tiger, the tabby cat, and voiced the feelings of them all.

'It's a crime,' he said bitterly. 'A bloody awful crime.'

The telephone call was for Dai. One of Josh Johnson's Shires had managed to kick the end off the electric fence and free himself, and had galloped over the moor, and was bogged down in mud. The fire brigade were there with tackle to pull him out. Dai was needed. He had noticed Josh's absence, which was rare.

The Huntsman took the rotor arm and promised to see that Steve did not drive himself home. Dai was glad to leave. There was nothing he could do, no comfort he could offer, and he too would suffer if the valley were flooded, as his home was uncomfortably near to Deep Willows, and might well be covered when the water was let in. He had no idea how much ground a new reservoir would cover, or how deep it would be in the end.

22

The flood water sometimes came as far as the end of his garden, but the ground sloped steeply and the house stood high and dry. It would take time. It would mean change. Dams would have to be built and men come to the area to work, and noise would come to the fells. And then desolation, with only water to replace houses and people and families.

Josh Johnson's lurcher, Bitty, greeted Dai with a sharp bark, and streaked over the moor, looking for her master, who had sent her home, as her anxiety was making her a nuisance. Dai raced after her, cursing the uneven ground and the thin moon which gave too little light and did not reveal potholes and ridges and tussocks until he had tripped over them.

Flood lights revealed the men working on the edge of the mud. Dai, looking down, saw the black head and white blaze and knew that this was Josh's champion, who had a will of his own and was often in trouble through it. Dai had run too fast. His heart raced and his pulses thumped and he gulped air that burned his throat. He watched the men fixing the ropes. Josh was on his knees in front of the terrified Shire, soothing him, and stroking him, praying that he would not struggle more and make rescue impossibly difficult. He had floundered and fallen in an isolated patch of bog, his weight forcing him deep. He was nine years old, splendidly built, heavily muscled, and champion stock. Three thousand pounds worth of horse sunk in muck to his withers. What bloody awful luck. One thing, the bog wasn't bottomless here. He'd go no lower. Cattle had gone in before and once Dai had helped rescue a hind that had trapped herself.

Dai walked over and bent down beside Josh. His work would begin when they had the stallion free. The animal would be filthy, soaked, and shocked. It would take most of the night to dry him and ensure that he suffered no ill. Dai hoped the Shire would be too feeble to rage when they worked on him. His name was Emperor, and he had a king-sized temper, and could never be groomed without a bluff over his eyes to blindfold him.

Josh was soon in the mud himself as no one else dared fix the ropes. The stallion might panic. He was quiet enough at the moment. He trusted Josh and seemed to understand that the men were trying to free him. Josh had stripped, and the wind's chilly fingers stroked his body. Dai leaned forward to give him a hand, and slipped. A moment later, he was on the other side of the horse, having decided that he was already so muddy it no longer mattered. The enclosing mire was bitter cold and he set his teeth. The stallion, partly consoled by the two men who now stood beside him, as deep in mud as he, quieted, and Dai groped beneath the animal for the ropes, and anchored them, praying the knots were fast and would not slip. Dai felt rock beneath his feet. They would not sink lower.

There was no chance of any vehicle driving over the ground. By now the firemen were augmented by a watching crowd, and willing hands took hold and tugged and pulled, and Josh and Dai thrust as hard as possible, until slowly, reluctantly, the bog gave up its prey. Dai had never known mud could be so glutinous. He was terrified of falling, lest he drown in slime. He and Josh had both been roped before they joined the stallion, but it was easy to fall sideways. Dai prayed that the ropes were strong. His foot slipped. He could imagine the mud round his nostrils, choking his throat, blinding his eyes, prey to sheer instinctive fear. The moonslip, rising clear over the wide bleak fells, was a mockery. An owl winged downwind, its lugubrious voice a fitting comment on the situation.

At last the stallion was safe. He lay, gasping and shaking, and, with two dexterous tugs, Dai and Josh stood beside him, both appreciating to the full how painful such a method of rescue must be for an animal. The ropes had tightened and they felt bruised and sore.

The Huntsman was armed with a bottle of whisky. He poured it into the stallion's mouth. The horse was too bewildered to protest. Life had assumed total unreality when ground that he had always known as solid betrayed him, and had given way.

It was lucky that, bored with freedom, he had been seeking his stable, and was not far from home. The men led him back. Emperor was too exhausted to protest. Normally he was a fine handful, arrogant with temper, and the only animal Dai had ever known that was not afraid of the electric fence. He had learned how to master it. Dai and Josh hastily dried themselves and changed into dry gear. Peg Johnson met them, saw their plight, and ran home, and came quickly to the stable with coffee laced with rum, and started working on the Shire while they drank.

Emperor was shivering. His massive head drooped. There was mud in his eyes and ears and his nostrils. His coat was plastered with mud. His massive feathered fetlocks were tangled, with a solid ball of muck around each leg. There could be no sleep tonight for any of them. Dai stayed to help. The Emperor was valuable, and Josh farmed single handed, Peg helping him whenever she could. There was never leisure for a farmer's wife on the fells.

By three in the morning Dai was working in his sleep. He had not slept much for nearly a week. Trouble always came chasing after trouble, and the blank spells rarely lasted long. Peg worked beside him, rubbing the mud away, trying to dry the animal, wondering if he would ever recover from such prolonged immersion. He had been bogged in icy mud for several hours. Rescue was never easy, and there was the risk of hurting the horse.

Peg, Josh's wife, was tall and well built, her thick unruly hair now grey. Dai often thought Peg's eyes the most remarkable he had seen, large, dark, and expressive as an animal's. She was a hard worker. A few minutes before four, when day was a dim rumour, she flung down the straw she was using to dry the horse, and went to make more coffee, hot and black and strong, her eyes feeling as if the lids were glued together.

The dogs greeted her affectionately and she quieted them. Dai examined the stallion. He was still very wet, but nothing they could do would dry him faster now. Josh had plugged a fan heater into a corner of the stable, but there was so much of Emperor. Nearly eighteen hands of solid Shire. No use attempting to clean the hair above his hooves, or his mane or tail, until much later. It would be a long difficult job, and the poor animal needed rest.

The coffee was bitter, and suddenly Dai remembered that he had not eaten. Hunger was an added penance, along with lack of sleep. Peg, discovering a few minutes later that Dai had not been home for his supper, went back to the kitchen and made ham sandwiches, for which he was extremely grateful.

She brought towels from the house and the three of them set

about the horse once more. Emperor, exhausted, wet, and miserable, was quiet as a child's riding pony, aware that they were trying to make him more comfortable. Light was creeping over the fells before Josh and Dai were satisfied. They piled straw loosely over the horse's back, and fastened a rug on top, ensuring that air could get through to finish the task of drying him.

Peg brought fresh bedding, and tedded it thick beneath the Shire. She made a warm mash, and the three of them were delighted when Emperor fed. He was still shivering. Dai examined him again carefully, but there was no sign of any damage. It would be necessary to keep an eye on him for some time, as prolonged chill might induce pneumonia. The vet sighed, and rubbed his eyes, longing for bed. One thing, Josh knew as much as any man alive about horses, and Dai had no need to worry on that score.

'Sleep for an hour in our kitchen, or you'll be off the road into the bog again,' Peg suggested. It was a good idea. He could not possibly drive home now, feeling as he did. He sat by the banked fire and fell asleep almost immediately.

Josh stretched in the sagging leather chair opposite him, while Peg went to lie on the bed for a brief spell. It would soon be milking time, and it was impossible to leave the cattle till later, as the lorry would be along for the churns.

The alarm clock wakened them all to misery. Aching, stiff, and longing for more sleep, Dai went back to the stable. Emperor, restored to interest, turned his head and whinnied, and Dai filled a haynet and left the horse tugging at it. Josh was already bringing in the cows for milking. Dai lifted an exultant thumb and Josh's grin of relief creased his leathery face.

Peg cooked bacon and eggs, made bitter black coffee, and rang Sheila to tell her that Dai was on his way home and would not need breakfast. Dai ate and drank in a daze. Surgery would be delayed this morning, as it was a longish drive back, and he needed a bath and a change of clothes. He yawned, and walked to the door, and looked over the fells.

There was a mist lying over the ground, hanging low, the sun gleaming on its surface so that it shimmered and danced and softened the landscape, and masked Horton Lake. Dai looked up at the hills. The peaks were harsh against the sky. He glanced across the valley, hidden and secret, watery mist lying everywhere, so that he saw the wide acres drowned and the farms only a memory. Deep Willows and Sheerlings, and the cottages, and Josh and his Bruton Shires would vanish, as if they had never been. And where would their owners go, Dai wondered.

A curlew in the ghostly distance trilled its soft plaintive cry, and Dai knew that only desolation could come to those uprooted and thrust out of their homes. The other day he had read in the morning paper of a farmer evicted by the motorway; the man had been awarded ample compensation, but compensation did not find a vacant farm, nor replace familiar animals sold because there was nowhere to keep them. Men tended to think that money bought lives and bought souls, and was the answer to every problem. Men had been glibly jubilant because the farmer had more than enough money on which to retire and live in comfort, but there was no pleasure away from beasts; there was no interest without a calving cow, or a foaling horse, or a milking herd. He was the last of long generations of farmers, and his life was his satisfaction, and he had no desire to change. Such men were always casualties of progress.

There was no purpose in the empty days; no joy in life without beasts of all kinds around; without his cattle and their individual tricks and traits and endless interest. There was no purpose in living, and one morning he walked over the despoiled fields where once he had tended his cows, and had raised a pedigree herd, and had taken out the champion who had won at the last Show, and groomed her for stardom. He looked at the straight bleak road along which cars now sped, which had replaced the friendly acres, and pulled the trigger of his gun. They found him lying beside the motorway that had destroyed his life. They could not understand what had gone wrong. The man had no money worries. They brought in a verdict of suicide while of unsound mind, and only Dai, who knew him well, and had tended his sick animals, realized that in those last moments, the farmer had been overwhelmed by the abysmal bleakness that comes with the destruction of a lifelong ambition.

The mist lifted. Sun shone on the fox-red bracken and glittered on the lake, and the vision vanished. The valley was not yet spoiled, and if he had his way, it never would be. They would fight, all of them, to retain their heritage.

Let drinking water come from the sea, from barriers built as the Dutch built, and not by flooding homes and farmland, by ruining lives that depended on the farmland. People mattered, everywhere, and not only those that lived in the cities. The country people had rights, too. But where, in God's name, did you begin?

Dai shook his head. He was stupid with tiredness. He climbed into the Land-Rover. Inside the farm kitchen the telephone rang insistently and Josh went to answer it. He came out again almost immediately.

'Sheila says that Steve's just phoned. Charity's calving, and he's tried to bring the calf but he can't. He wants you to go over.'

Dai said nothing. He let in the clutch and prayed for strength. He was so tired he felt stupid, and stupidity killed more beasts than intelligence. He was too alone. He must get a partner, and find some time to sleep, if nothing else. There was rarely time to read, to keep up with advances made in the last few years, to discuss improvements in technique, to exchange experiences. There was rarely time for Sheila, or for the children, or for himself. A day's fishing, sitting under a tree, watching the sun shimmer on running water, and a dipper preen on a stone, and hearing nothing but wind noise and bird call, that would be luxury beyond price.

Now even thought was a luxury and Charity needed him, poor beast. He had no eye for the fells, or the lake, or the cloud shadows fleeting across the hills. The wind from the sea chased away the last memory of night, hurling itself against the Land-Rover, threatening it with its power. Dai concentrated on steering, and was thankful when he turned the corner that led to Deep Willows and saw Steve waiting at the gate. Lysbeth was as good as any vet with a calving cow, so long as there were no complications, and she had stayed in the byre, while her husband looked anxiously for the vet. Dai flung open the Land-Rover door, and jumped down.

28

CHAPTER FOUR

DAI walked into the cowshed. There were times when he envied hospital surgeons, working under sterile conditions, while he battled in a primitive building, with makeshift lights, and muck all round him. A human patient could also be spoken to, and reassured, but no one could tell a sick animal or a beast in pain that it would soon feel better, that the misery would ease tomorrow, that the men around were trying to help. As far as the animal knew, the men were there to compound its misery, and terror at the unknown forces that racked its body drove many a quiet animal frantic.

Charity had been restless for hours, tramping round her stall. Steve had moved her to a shed that he kept specially for difficult calvings. Dai was always thankful when he had to work at Deep Willows, as the lights were good and the place as clean as possible, the walls whitewashed, the floor hosed down and spread with clean straw. The cow had become badly unsettled during the night, and her long bellows of misery dominated the farm. The dogs sat, uneasy, having been told to be quiet, but their eyes followed every movement that the men made, as if they could not understand why they did nothing for the cow, to help her out of her obvious agony.

Dai examined Charity. She was showing signs of exhaustion. The membranes had ruptured some time before, but the calf was no nearer birth. He inserted his hand slowly, and felt the lie of the calf. He had not examined her closely before. He stood, thinking, his fingers exploring gently, his mind going over all the cases he had dealt with in the past, temporarily blind and deaf to everything around him, as he tried to computerize the facts in his brain, and to decide what was best for the animal. Steve, standing by Charity's head, spoke to her softly, but she was beyond all comfort, and again and again the loud bellow disturbed the other animals, and saddened the morning.

Lysbeth, knowing the cow was in better hands than hers, went off to cope with the delayed chores.

Dai's exploring hand felt a second leg, and then, bewilderingly, no head at all. For one horrible moment he visualized a monster, as the legs were moving and the calf was obviously alive. A moment later his hand encountered the little beast's tail, and he realized that it was the wrong way round. The calf lay backwards.

The problem was far from easy. Steve had the calving rope ready, and was long experienced, so that it was soft and clean and had been well soaked in antiseptic solution. Dai fixed it carefully. By now Stan Turner, the cattle manager, had finished his jobs with the rest of the herd and come to help. It would be necessary to pull the calf from the cow.

Gently, gently, pullee calfee, Dai thought, suddenly thinking of Mollie who, when younger, had found Conker, her pony, a handful to catch and had said, 'Softly, softly, catchee pony', so often that the whole family began to invent new catchwords. Tim, one morning, woke them by yelling, 'Quickee, quickee, Deedee sickee', and Susie's latest was 'Hushee, hushee, Daddy maddie', which Dai had to admit, ruefully, applied only too often these days. He was always too damn' tired.

He hastily switched his mind back to the cowshed, to the bellowing cow, to the two men pulling gently, and patiently, carefully, but strongly, on the ropes, while he balanced Charity, who was leaning her weight against him. He was filthy again, smothered in blood and dung, as well as mud from the night before, as the Shire had leaned against him as he had dried him. Sheila would have a pile of washing.

Time was running away with them. The calf might die. Time was speeding, and yet the minutes seemed endless, and they dared not hurry, or they would injure mother and calf. Dai had forgotten everything but the task in hand. His eyes watched Charity, and the rope that seemed not to be moving at all. At least the legs were now straight. The long mournful bellows were part of the background, and if they ever stopped he would find life too silent. Charity's anguished voice reminded Stan Turner, who had once lived on the coast, of the sound of a foghorn over the bay, as a ship nosed through the mist, seeking a landfall.

There was a sudden movement. The calf came free, and Dai caught it and lowered it to the straw. It was appallingly still. Steve and Stan began to work on the cow, and Dai knelt beside the tiny red and white Hereford calf, and cleared its nose and mouth. There was still no sign of breathing. He lifted it by the hind legs and slapped it vigorously, thankful that Charity was too exhausted to protest. Had she been fit, she might well have attacked him, sure that he was damaging her offspring. There was still no breath in its small body.

Dai laid it in the straw again, and knelt beside it, and began to rub, using wisped straw, and all his strength. The door of the shed was ajar. Steve's collie bitch sat beside it, watching. Bess loved all young animals, and came in to look at the calf. Her soft tongue began to lick the calf's neck. Dai glanced up. Charity had been led to the shelter of the stall and was out of sight. The collie continued to lick.

The calf gasped in air. A few seconds later, it was breathing steadily, and one ear flickered. Dai began to dry the little animal as Charity was too exhausted to start mothering immediately. The collie helped him, enthusiastic, delighted to have a young creature to care for again. Steve always had to banish her when the other bitches had pups, as she tried to adopt them, and there was trouble.

Lysbeth had taken over Steve's jobs for the morning. She came into the shed with coffee for the three of them, and bent to caress Bess, and to admire the calf, which was shaking its head and moving its legs, its eyes roaming over the people who surrounded it. Charity bellowed again, as the cleansing came free, and Stan lifted the calf and took it to her.

The cow had had five calves in her lifetime, and motherhood was an intense pleasure. The bellowing quieted as she looked down at the tiny creature lying in the straw. She bent and nosed it, and the small head turned to meet her, and the little beast stared up at the cow above her, looming, immense. Scent filled her nose; warm, comforting, and right, and she tried to stand and reach her. Stan Turner put down a hand, and at once the small mouth fastened on his finger and tried to suck.

'I say it every time,' Stan said, 'and it still beats me. How the hell do they always know?'

Dai watched Charity lick her calf. There was delight in her

31

eyes, and pride. Already the birth pangs were no more than a vague memory, and, on the straw beside her, was her greatest achievement, the meaning of her existence. Steve stood looking at them, gloating. He might have produced the calf himself. This was total satisfaction.

Dai drank his coffee, well content. An awkward problem had been solved, a new challenge met, and here to prove it were a live cow and a healthy calf. The little animal was almost on its feet, and Stan held it, and guided its head to the cow's udder, while Charity watched every movement, and her warm tongue licked along her small daughter's back. Steve grinned at Dai, jubilant. Another heifer. Another future mother for the milking herd, another prize beast, another solid, tangible achievement. Steve was almost as proud of the calf as Charity.

'No problems there.'

Dai grinned back and nodded, thankful. The first suckling was vital, the milk immediately after birth containing the life-promoting colostrum that ensured that the calf's digestive system began to function adequately. Without it there was real trouble, and unless the little animal could suckle properly there were more problems for the cowman too, as it could not be left to overcome its own difficulties. It needed his help.

'Hey, hey,' Steve said suddenly. 'Calf bed's coming adrift.'

Dai jumped to attention. He had been congratulating himself too early. He turned back into the shed. Sometimes after the birth was over the cow expelled her uterus, and trying to push it in again was like trying to thread rug wool into a fine-eyed needle. A few stitches would prevent that. Dai blessed Stan's quick eyes. Steve always said his cow manager was worth ten times his salary, and Stan proved it time and time again. Hours of work had been saved. Stan removed the cleansing, and took it to the incinerator, while Steve supervised the calf, and watched Charity and held her still, and Dai inserted the stitches.

'At least she's had her beastings,' Stan said a few minutes later, as the calf, worn out by its first attempt at suckling, dropped back into the straw.

The foreman's name for colostrum was an odd one, and Dai, now sure that all was well, walked out into the yard, pondering the country names for so many country things. It was never easy to change from one part of Britain to another, as each county seemed to have its own names for its own beasts. Dai had often seen the notices of Scottish sheep sales advertising 'thieves' for sale but had never discovered what a 'thief' was, and no one hereabouts knew either.

He drove home, hoping that there had been no emergencies waiting. A brief word with his wife over the telephone confirmed that everyone knew that there would be an extra surgery, at two that afternoon, to make up for the loss of the morning. There were several animals undergoing a course of injections. One of them was a large Alsatian that had unwisely tried to leap a barbed wire fence and gashed his chest, giving himself a jagged infected wound. Sully, the baker's boxer, could not be left until tomorrow, and neither could the cat from the Swan, who had been bitten by a rat that she had unwisely tackled. The brute was large and fat and had inflicted savage damage on Tiger's hind paw. The local rats were all immune to Warfarin and that was an added worry. There were always rats around farms, and too few owls, and hawks, and kestrels, to fight them. Stoats, and weasels, and foxes, also kept the plague at bay. It didn't do to check nature. She always got her own back in the end.

It was good to think of the calving. Dai never tired of birth, and familiarity never dimmed the exultation of seeing a healthy mother and a healthy little beast beside her. No matter how often he officiated, there was always something different; something new; some endearing gesture from the dam or the young, and there was always the sense of achievement, of reward, of saving a life, and doing so under circumstances that would make any surgeon gag.

He was grinning as he climbed down from the Land-Rover, but the smile died as he saw his wife's face.

'Trouble?'

Before Sheila could answer, Susie, at home because of half-term, ran at him, and pummelled him furiously with her fists, shouting.

'You're not to. You're not to. You're not to!'

Mucky though he was, he lifted the child and held her close, and her fury dimmed and died in stifled uncontrollable sobs.

33

'What on earth's happened?' he asked.

Sheila sighed.

'There's a black Persian queen waiting for you to spay her and put her four-day-old kittens down,' she said. 'She was brought in this morning, and the old fool who brought her came into the kitchen, instead of the waiting-room. She gave her to Tim with a message, and Susie saw the cat and the kits.'

Elation died. Dai set down the child and walked indoors, anger choking him. Damn people. Damn all people. He did not enjoy killing kittens at the best of times, but if he killed these now that Susie had seen them, there would be hell to pay. He had only done so once before, and the child had cried herself sick, had developed a temperature, and had refused to go near him for nearly a week, making him feel perpetually like a murderer. Susie was passionate about all animals. He just couldn't face upsetting her so badly again. If only the woman had gone to the waiting-room, and rung for Sheila. The children were not allowed in that part of the house.

He walked into the annexe beside the surgery. The black Persian was stretched in a box lined with one of the children's jerseys. Her kittens were suckling, and her tongue licked them devotedly. She looked up at Dai, her green eyes proud, and purred, the sound throbbing. Her world was all delight.

Sheila came into the room and stood beside him, looking down.

'God damn the owner,' Dai said bitterly. 'I think he must have slipped up sadly when he made the human race. Why didn't she have her spayed first? And why did she have to come into the private part of the house?'

Sheila could say nothing. She had had to rear so many young animals in the Zoo that it seemed criminal to destroy any, even though her common sense acknowledged the necessity. They shut the door on the cat. There was nothing to be said, and they let her enjoy her kittens while she could.

Dai went up to have a bath and change, but all the pleasure had gone from the day.

CHAPTER FIVE

DAI lay, delighting in warmth. Sheila had taken away his dirty clothes and brought clean ones, and there was added pleasure in knowing that soon he would be dressed in fresh linen. He propped the mirror on the end of the bath and shaved thoughtfully, thinking about the Persian cat. If only people would have cats spayed. Dai had found homes for more kittens than he could remember, and now there was a new problem. The Persian cat reminded him of it.

Bess Logan had brought this particular matter to his notice only two days before. Bess was old and crotchety and some said she was a witch and born of witches. The bent, little, grey-haired, old woman knew many country remedies for both human and animal ills, and her knowledge of herbs and healing plants and soothing drinks was extensive. Her cough cures were preferred by many to the doctor's; yet, in spite of that, if a cow sickened, or a calf died, there were still those among the very old who believed that Bess had cast a spell on them, and who spat at her to avert the evil eye.

Bess did not care. She lived alone, and at first had only one cat for company, but when she called Dai in to share a pot of tea, and to look at Sam's ear, as he was wearing it oddly, flat against his skull, shaking his head, and she suspected canker, he found seven cats in her sitting-room.

'Are you boarding them, Bess?' he asked.

Bess had been storing her anger, and it suddenly erupted.

Behind her home was Brickmill Lane, which had been a village headache for long enough. The villagers used the grass verges to dump their unwanted rubbish; prams and bedsteads and old mattresses, made the lane sordid, and kept the council busy sending carts at intervals to take the stuff away. The cottages were an eyesore, tumbledown, damp, dirty, with paper peeling from the walls, roofs that leaked, a single cold

35

water tap in the yard and an earth closet at the end of the yard. Nobody tended the weedy overgrown patches of earth that were graced by the name of garden. As tenants died the cottages were left empty. The landlord died, leaving no relatives. At last there was a re-housing order, and everyone moved to high-storey flats in Horton, where no pets were allowed. The dogs all went to Dai. He kept one and found it a home with the postman and put down four that were over ten years old, and would not have taken kindly to new owners.

The families had left their cats behind. For some reason, cats were thought to enjoy living wild, and often left to fend for themselves. Yet a cat could be as affectionate as a dog, given a good owner; an owner the animal could trust; an owner who cared for its comfort, and kept it fed, and warm, and well housed. Bess had been unable to bear to see the forlorn creatures foraging for themselves, growing thin, and wild, and breeding among the rubble of the deserted cottages.

She had taken them all in, and was trying to keep them on the tiny pension that was barely enough for her own needs. Dai had not realized that the two tom-cats that she had brought in recently to be neutered had not belonged to neighbours unable to bring them, as she said, but to Bess. Had he known, he'd have done the job free, but Bess had forestalled him. She'd always been proud and she knew how he would react if he knew the truth.

Dai had looked the cats over; black and white, grey, tabby, all were curled comfortably, and the room burred with their concerted purrs. Bess kept her home immaculate, and it and the cats were spotless. Bess groomed them, and they trusted her, and rubbed against her. Later that day, when Dai exploded to his wife about the stupidity of people, Sheila took the old woman a carton of tins of cat-food, and, on her way home, stopped her veteran station wagon outside the butcher's and cajoled him into promising to send Bess pieces and trimmings and bones. The fishmonger, too, knowing Sheila, yielded readily. No one could argue with the vet's wife when her mind was made up. Bess and her cats would be cared for.

But there would soon be other problems, as the old row of houses in Back Lane, in Bruton-under-the-Water, was also due to be demolished. Dai determined to visit each house and note what beasts were kept, and ensure that none was left alone to fret, bewildered by desertion by a family it had learned to trust. Perhaps he could ensure that either they had new homes, or were given a painless death. Life was easier in a small place where everyone knew everyone else. Those living in cities were always defeated by the sheer size of a problem. He remembered the mangy miserable cats he had seen in Rome. His thoughts were abruptly interrupted.

'You'd best hurry, Dad.' Tim put his head round the bath-room door. 'There are already two people waiting and Mum says you're not starting work till you've eaten.'

Dai climbed out of the bath, dried himself and dressed hastily. The racing clock mocked him as he went into the surgery, and called the first patient in, thankful, after a quick glance round the waiting-room, to see that there were only minor complaints. The black Persian haunted him. Every time he looked at her she purred in delight, sure he was admiring her family, and proud beyond measure to show off her kits. She had never known motherhood before. Last time he had gone into the study Susie had been kneeling beside her, stroking the black fur. She looked at her father defiantly, knowing she should not be there, and ran off. There was no question of killing those kittens.

At last work was over. There were no more calls to make; no emergencies; no impatient telephone bells signalling disaster. Dai shared the children's tea, carefully avoiding the subject of the black Persian. Susie, knowing the cat was still nursing her kittens, and aware too that the longer her father delayed, the less likely he was to put them to sleep, relaxed, and came to sit on the settee beside Dai and curl herself against him, needing, as always, the reassurance of his arms.

It was rare luxury to hold the child, and watch an indifferent and amateurish television performance, and think of nothing. Mollie was sewing, making a skirt for herself. The work was going badly. She hated needlework, and her deep sighs made Deedee stare, her head cocked on one side, one ear up and one ear down, intrigued by the odd sounds. Rusty lay on the hearth-rug, mesmerized by the flames. Dai often wondered if the fox hankered for the wild, and once he had released him. But Rusty had never known freedom. He thought he had been banished,

37

and he arrived home before Dai, and sat at the gate waiting. Now no one remembered he was a fox and not a dog.

Tia and Sim were curled together beside Susie. Sheila had gone to feed the patients and check that all was well. Television irritated Sheila. She preferred to read when she had time to spare, which was seldom. Tim, seated on the window seat, was staring into a night made wild by wind, clouds whipping across the moon, the trees surging and swooping as the gale took them and played with them. Shifting shadows startled the Great Dane, who had come to stand beside him and stare out into the mysterious darkness. Deedee, now fully grown, was massively made, yet totally elegant. She leaned her head on Tim's knee. She needed people.

Sheila, coming into the room, glanced at the clock.

'Nearly eight. That's not bad going. I've finished. Where's Mark?'

'I thought he was with you,' Dai said lazily. He was almost asleep, comfortably warm, the words of the television play drifting into his mind without registering.

'I haven't seen him since tea,' Sheila said. 'See if he's in his room, Tim.'

Tim vanished, to reappear a few minutes later.

'He's not been up there at all. It's too tidy. And where's Elliott?'

Elliott was never missing from an evening round the fire. He woke up at dusk, and was transformed into a quicksilver demon, his games with shoelaces and Susie's pigtails enlivening everyone. It was astonishing that no one had missed his small but vigorous presence.

Dai switched off the television set.

'Bed, Susie,' he said. 'The rest of you come and see if we can find Mark.'

By nine o'clock, Dai was really anxious, and Sheila was frantic. They had scoured the garden, calling, and hunted through coachhouse and stables. There was no sign of Elliott, and none at all of Mark.

By now, rain was tipping out of a sky dark with massed cloud, and the wind screamed eerily round the house. The trees, creaking and groaning, disturbed Mollie, who hated wind. She went indoors. Mark had never stayed out before. Mollie would have liked to join in the search, but someone had to stay with Susie, and Mollie knew her mother would be better occupied. Sitting, waiting and wondering, was total misery. Oh, Mark, Mark, she thought, you little ass, where are you? She put her arms round her small sister, reassuring the child, but she did not believe her own words, and listened bleakly to the wind as it howled in the chimney.

Sheila telephoned two of Mark's friends, neither of whom had seen him. She came out to stand by Dai, huddled into her raincoat. Visions of one disaster after another crowded upon her. Tim was always cautious, but Mark was reckless, never thinking until too late, so that it was Mark who climbed the old wall after a kestrel's nest, just to see inside, and fell when the wall collapsed under his weight. It was Mark who climbed down beside the river to rescue a lamb, and could not climb back again. Luckily the shepherd's collie barked a warning, and Mark had been rescued.

Dai whistled to Deedee and told her to find Mark. She could track anything, but could she track tonight on wet ground, in the wind and the rain? All scent would be washed away. He flashed his torch. Where the dickens could the boy have gone?

Deedee quartered the ground, hunting, hopefully, but there were traces of Mark everywhere, and she was bewildered. She cast, and cast again, and then, baffled, sat in front of Dai and howled her discouragement. She did not know where to look, and the wind drowned all sound. She sat in the rain, defeated, and Dai stood beside her, anxiety paramount.

'I've phoned the Swan,' Sheila said. 'They're all coming to help us look. Dai, where is he?'

Dai had no answer. Mark was totally unpredictable. He was fearless, confident, and unaware of danger. One thing Dai was certain about, was that where Mark was, Elliott was also, as both were missing. He looked at the trees that soared over the garden wall, and beyond them, those surrounding the church. Elliott had never tried to climb and had not discovered trees as yet, but if he did, he would most certainly, as did all the kittens, climb too high, and get stuck. Sim had been stuck in the rafters. And it was Mark who had climbed after him and brought him down, although he was only seven at the time. Sim had been old enough to know better, but cats loved climbing.

The wind snatched at Dai's hair and snatched away his voice. If Mark had climbed on a night like this, he would surely have fallen. Fear was unknown to the child, but Dai, remembering other folks' tragedies, shivered. There was nothing he could do but search again. Beyond the walls the river roared in anger, swollen by rain that had fallen in the mountains. The river was over its banks on the ground beyond Sheerlings, where the Wellans had farmed for centuries. It was over its banks at Deep Willows too. Both old farmhouses were threatened by the rising water. Dai had a sudden vision of the valley when the reservoir was built. He changed the word to 'if'. It was not a pleasant thought, but was less worrying than wondering what had happened to Mark. Or was it?

Deedee pressed against his leg. Tim, standing beside him, stared into the darkness, straining his ears. There was nothing but the din of the wind, the swish, and thrust, and roar and surge of the trees, and the terrifying thunder of the rolling boulders in the river bed, tossed high by water raging from the hills.

The first headlights, cutting through the darkness, were more welcome than Dai could have believed possible, and the voices of men spilling from the cars, and running towards him, were reassurance. These were his friends, his people. He knew them all, had tended their beasts, had helped in their disasters and now they had come to help him. He could not speak, but their presence warmed him.

Before half an hour had passed, there were twenty men and seven dogs congregated outside the House of Beasts. The last to arrive was Sergeant Henty from Horton with the news that two radio cars were on their way. The men went off, shouting Mark's name, to comb the garden again, and hunt on the fells. None of them mentioned the river, which now deafened them all, its roar ominous. If Mark had been there when it came into spate . . . Ned Foley listened to the water. He knew, better than any, the surge, and swift thrust, and swirl as the first torrents rushed from the mountains, so that the stream which, a few minutes before, had been churtling gently over boulders, was transformed into a hellbound thrashing mass of stormy water, white with foam, dark with peat brought down in its anger, taking to itself any beast or man that happened to be in its way.

There had been two campers the year before, drowned when the island flooded. And the old shepherd from Burtonskille, caught unaware as he crossed the bridge to his home. The spate always came with a bore that swept everything before it. The river had taken the bridge that night, as well as a car that had been driving along the river road, and numbered three deaths on its tally.

Mark was a favourite of Ned's, more so than the other children. Mark loved to visit the old man, now settled in a house near the Swan. Once he had lived rough on the fells, but age and authority had forced him into more civilized ways, and old bones were thankful for four walls and a warm hearth. Ned was a reformed character. The lad listened to his stories of the beasts on the fells, and went fishing with him during the school holidays. Mark was a grand little fisherman. Where in God's name was the boy?

CHAPTER SIX

MARK was an active child, who quickly tired of indoor ploys. He rarely walked, but raced everywhere, a characteristic that twice involved him in accidents at school, as he tore round a corner and met another boy headlong. The first time he lost two teeth, the second he bit through lip and tongue, and the other boy smashed his nose into Mark's forehead, so that the two of them arrived at the school First Aid room looking as if murder had been attempted.

Only Ned Foley could curb Mark's hurry, as patience was needed to watch beasts in the wild, and, with Ned, Mark remembered to be quiet and gentle. He reacted afterwards against the necessary restraint by racing against Deedee, or climbing a tree that challenged him by its height, and, until Dai discovered him and showed his anger forcefully, by diving into the river and swimming under water in the deep pools, to see how long he could hold his breath. Swimming and climbing alone were now forbidden. He might get cramp, or be caught in weed, or hurt himself with no one there to help; or he might slip, swarming up a tree, and the very least he could hope for, falling from such a height, was a broken limb. He might break his neck.

The embargo irritated Mark. He made up for it by climbing in the barn and coachhouse. Here, all was fairly safe, and if he fell he would fall on straw. He had a wide collection of books on mountaineering, bought with saved pocket money, and one day he intended to climb properly.

That night he had gone out into the yard, and found Elliott hiding from the rain under an upturned wheelbarrow, unable to get into the house because no one had heard him above the sound of the wind. Out here, Elliott's yowl, inherited from his mother, brought him speedy attention, and Mark lifted the kitten and carried him indoors, intending to take the little animal up to his room and play with him. He glanced into the sitting-room. His mother was not there, and everyone else seemed engrossed in the television play. Mark did not care for television. The programmes bored him. He sat on the stairs for some minutes, wondering what to do with himself. It was too wet and too windy to go outside.

There were several trunks in the attic. He remembered that he had put some of his own treasures up there, things his mother said he no longer needed, as he had outgrown them. tried to remember just what was in the trunks. He had a project to do for school. The Romans in the Lake District. It particularly appealed to him, as Dai was interested in Roman history, and, when he had time, told the children about the Legions, and the Eagles, fascinating them with his tales. There might be some useful books or magazines. Many of Dai's back copies of *Nature*, and his out-of-date veterinary publications, were stored there, as well as some of the household books. Sheila thought that there were some history books among them.

The attics were rarely visited. The narrow, twisting stairs were covered in cheap carpet. The four rooms were a warren, one leading out of another, tucked beneath the rafters. Once, when people were wealthier than now, they had been the servants' quarters, stifling in summer, and freezing in winter. The windows were tiny and let in little light. The House of Beasts was old. How old, nobody quite knew.

Mark flicked a switch, and the bare electric light bulb revealed a welter of rubbish. Old tin trunks; and suitcases; a broken tennis racket, most of its strings gone; a hockey stick, cracked at the top, that Sheila had condemned as dangerous; a parrot cage, put away after its inmate had died, when Mark was very small. He could still remember Poll, whose main comment on life was 'Stone me! It's freezing', no matter what the weather. It caused great entertainment when Poll announced he was freezing in the middle of a heat wave, and the remark was now part of the family history, used as a joke on hot days, much to the mystification of outsiders who had never known the parrot.

Elliott was entranced. He could hide behind the trunks; he could play with the suitcases; he could find odd pieces of string and track them. He discovered a pile of tissue paper, and leaped into it, hunting through the rustles frantically, sure they must be caused by a mouse.

Two days before, he had nearly caught his first mouse, missing it only by inches, and he was determined to find one for himself and not have to play with Sim's cast-offs. He liked playing, but Sim and Tia soon tired of games, and Elliott's brothers and sisters had been given away, and were enchanting new owners, who had not needed much persuasion to have cats for the first time. Deedee and Rusty were much too rough.

Mark rustled the paper, and Elliott startled himself by jumping straight through it. Mark stooped to catch him, and Elliott rolled on his back, and fought the boy's hand, biting in mock ferocity, kicking with both hind legs against his wrist. It was a game that all cats loved, but it had to be watched, lest excitement made them spiteful. Both Sim and Tia knew when to stop, and kicked with sheathed hind claws, but Elliott was carried away, and ripped Mark's arm. Mark sucked at the scratches, and Elliott, exhilarated with joy, raced up a ladder in the corner of the room, and found himself under the skylight. One corner of it had been broken, long ago, and covered with plywood and forgotten. The plywood had rotted under the broken glass, and Elliott saw the darkness of the sky through the gap, and the shine on the roof.

The rain had eased, and dark was calling. Dark was a delirium of joy, was forbidden delight, as there were foxes on the fells, who sometimes prowled the garden, creeping through unknown holes, hunting for food that the animals had left. The children lost a rabbit to them, and a kitten vanished, the tracks on the ground in the morning revealing the killer. Now all cats stayed inside at nightfall, and Elliott had never been allowed to experience its wild allure.

His absence had been overlooked that evening. Sheila usually checked to see that he was indoors, but Susie had been persistently irritating, bothering about the Persian kittens, and her mother had forgotten. He had not liked the rain, but now the showers were over, and he was eager to explore.

Elliott was entranced. He could smell the night, and he was high, higher than he had ever been, and could go even higher. Mark looked up from the book that he had found just in time to

44

see the little cat's tail vanishing through the skylight on to the roof.

He ran up the ladder. The skylight was stiff, and it was not easy to push it open. The bolts were rusty and hard to undo, but at last he managed to force it up sufficiently to squeeze through the gap. Elliott was climbing towards the roof ridge, and Mark was sure the kitten would slip and fall. He might slip too. He shed his shoes, and clambered on to the tiles. The skylight slammed shut behind him. He tried to push his hand through the wood, but only one corner of it had gone, just enough to allow a kitten to slip through. He could not force his arm in far enough to open it. He could not lift it from the outside. He could not get back, as Dai had boarded over the glass, and completely covered it, and the frame was flush, fitting tightly.

Mark sat on the roof, and wondered what on earth he could do. Elliott reached the stack, and leaned against it, savouring the warmth. Suppose the kitten climbed on top of the chimney? Suppose he fell, as the birds sometimes fell in the nesting season? He would go straight into the log fire that was blazing below and be burnt alive. The thought was unbearable. Mark launched himself up the steep slope towards the kitten, reaching him just as Elliott began to clamber higher, using the rough brickwork as leverage for his claws. Mark could not shout down the chimney as the stack was too high for him to climb. He tried, but the holds were too slight, and he was hampered by Elliott.

He tucked the kitten inside his shirt and fastened the buttons. Elliott was wet and his fur was clammy, but at least he was safe. Mark turned to climb down. The wind surged against him, flattening him, and rain poured from the sky as if it had been flung from a giant bucket. As he moved, his foot slipped, and he realized that the steep roof had turned into a deathslide. His only hope was to crouch against the chimney stack and hang on tight.

He was cold. He was wet. He was frightened. Elliott, after an initial struggle, curled up and went to sleep. He at least was warm, and out of the wind. Mark could do nothing. He tried shouting, but he dared not stand, the stack was high, his voice was blown away to merge with the din of the gale, and no one

45

heard. He could only wedge himself firmly into the angle where the bricks met the roof, and huddle close against it for warmth, the hope that they would find him. But they would not know where to look. He had nothing with him that would make a light. If only he had a torch. If only he had a match, but matches would be blown out in this wind. If only he could find something in his pockets, and drop it, and attract attenion, but all he had was an end of string, a filthy handkerchief, and half a bar of chocolate that a girl at school had given him. Janet Dee. Mark rather thought she fancied him. He didn't like her much, but he liked chocolate. He ate it thoughtfully. He wondered if he could write a message in chocolate on the paper and throw it down, but it would only blow away. He resigned himself to wait out the long wet night, wondering if anyone had missed him.

He knew that they had when he saw the cars converging, their headlights cleaving the dark, clearly visible from a surprising distance. He had an astonishing view. He could see the isolated lights of farmhouses on the fells, the looped street-lamps of Bruton-under-the-Water, the tawny golden glow from the massed streets of Cantchester, far away to the West. Another glow showed where Horton lay, enfolded by mountains. He could see the trees, his eyes now acclimatized to darkness, and he watched them hurl themselves away from the wind, and bow and stretch again, and listen to the wild cacophony of sound that terrified the night.

Far below, he heard Deedee's bark, faint, remote, a ghost noise from an invisible dog. Fear nudged him. He could not see the ground. It was impossibly and frighteningly distant. He had only to slip, and he would crash down three storeys and lie, broken. He began to shiver, only partly with cold. He wished that he had worn his anorak, but who would expect to look for a book and end up on the roof? And his feet were cold and his socks were wet and he felt beastly. It might be better to take them off. He could not decide.

He could feel Elliott throbbing against him. The kitten was a small ball of warmth against the boy's chest, and Mark bent his head to listen, and heard the soft unmistakable sound of his purr. Elliott, you fool, Mark thought miserably. It was no use fretting. There was nothing whatever he could do. He would have to stay till morning, and hope that inspiration might come with daylight, or that the wind would drop so that he could yell. The wind gusted towards him, screeching, mocking him with its voice.

Below him the men fanned out, some towards the fells, some towards the river. Dai walked forlornly under the trees, looking up, wondering if Elliott had climbed and Mark climbed after him, and was marooned, terrified, in one of the elms. Mark saw the flashing torch searching the branches, and wished they would flash towards him. The rain was unending. He had never been so wet in his life, and now even Elliott was wet, and tried to get out of the damp by crawling under Mark's arm. The cat's yowl was sudden and unnerving, and Mark jumped. He wished the rain would stop. He wished he had never followed the kitten. He wished the skylight hadn't slammed, but wishing was useless. He cuddled closer to the stack. The fire had burned low, and the warmth vanished rapidly. Elliott, unhappy and uncomfortable, clung painfully, anchoring himself with small sharp claws, and Mark remembered the boy who had had a fox gnaw his vitals, and knew just how he felt. He had always thought it an absurd story and he couldn't remember the details, or remember who the boy was, or when he lived, or just why it had been necessary to cuddle a fox under his clothing. Maybe he'd been caught out too.

'Mind your claws, Elliott, you nut,' Mark said, just to reassure himself with the sound of his own voice. Elliott yowled again, irritably. He loathed wet.

The church clock called the endless quarters. Mark began to recite to himself, to pass the time away. He recited his tables; and the poem he had learned the week before; and a passage of Shakespeare that he had been set as a penance in detention. Most of it eluded him, but some of the words remained.

Friends, Romans, countrymen ... No one could forget that.

I come to bury Caesar, not to praise him. That, he was sure, was wrong. It sounded silly. He tried to think about Caesar, and Brutus helping to betray his friend. He did not like Shakespeare. The words were sometimes fine, but the teacher made it so boring.

47

He began to think instead about the black Persian. It belonged to old Mrs. Hicks, down at Green Spinney. He'd seen her bring it in. Mark hadn't known she had a cat. She'd never had one before and he was sure he'd heard the postmistress say that Mrs. Hicks disliked all animals. No wonder she'd brought the kittens to be destroyed, but why did she have a cat if she didn't like them? It was not a very profitable train of thought but it passed a few more minutes. Mark settled himself to ease cramped legs, watched the torches on the fells, and sighed miserably.

There were torches flashing everywhere. Mark could see one along the side of the river, gleaming on a froth of water that was boiling with foam. They must all be desperately worried, and here he was safe enough, and stupidly marooned. What a tomfool thing to do. And how everyone at school would laugh at daft old Mark Evans, lost all night on his own house roof. Nutty old Mark. How stupid could you get? Oh hell, Mark thought bitterly, why didn't I think and wedge the bally fanlight open?

One quarter rang from the church clock. A quarter to what? No, a quarter past what? Midnight? Three in the morning? He had forgotten what time the clock struck last.

He would think about his project. The Romans in the Lake District. He already knew something about that, as they had studied it at school. He had seen the Roman bath house at Ravenglass, and the hut circles on the road to Ulpha, that dated from pre-Roman times. He had visited part of Hadrian's wall, and seen the remains of the Roman fort at the top of Hardknott Pass. From there, a legionary must have been able to see almost the whole of the Lake District on a clear day. Perhaps little had changed since then over most of the country. But then there had been wolf and boar in Britain, and perhaps even bears. He could not remember. It would be queer to have to watch out for bears down by the river. Now there were only foxes and otters.

By the time dawn lightened the peaks, the men had come back to congregate in Dai's yard, and stand disconsolate. Dai's face was grey, and Sheila, making coffee, could not speak. All she could think of was Mark, out there, somewhere, God knew where, lost, freezing with cold and wet, perhaps with a broken leg or . . . But that was a thought she dared not pursue, nor dared she look at the river, now fattened with run-off from the hills and imbued with such fury that it sped faster than fox-flight towards Horton Lake.

Ned came to stand among the men, his mind on Mark. Mark could see the searchers now, could see the huddle of dark coats, and the glow and dim of a pipe, or cigarette. He looked at the roof about him. Perhaps he could prise off a tile and throw it down, and attract attention. But it might hit one of the men below, and the tiles were thick and heavy. There was nothing he could do. He tried to wave his arm, but gave up the effort. He was stiff and aching all over, so cold that his teeth chattered uncontrollably, and tears eased themselves down his cheeks. He had never been so miserable in his life. Only the small warmth of Elliott, now cuddled close against him, tired out with pro-testing, gave any comfort.

Susie could not sleep. Deedee was restless, and ran indoors several times and pawed at one or another of them in turn. It was Susie who looked at her thoughtfully.

'Deedee's trying to tell us something,' she said.

Tim looked at his sister impatiently. He was worried sick. Mark was an idiot, and always had been, and always would be, but all the same, he was Mark, and part of the family, and they had had good times together. Susie wouldn't realize how bad things were, and now she had to go on about the bally dog. Where in heaven was Mark?

Deedee, now desperate, raced about in frenzy, looking for Dai. She was his, and he usually understood her, but today he was being completely obtuse. She had known for some time exactly where to look for Mark and Elliott. She had been up-stairs, and found Mark's scent on the ladder that led to the roof. The boy and the kitten were out there. She could smell them in the room, and hear their small movements above her. She barked, bewildered by the reactions of her owners. She had never known them so stupid. No one heeded her attempts to attract attention. Dai, exhausted, was irritated by the bitch, who, instead of hunting through the grounds and on to the fells, as he expected, had persisted in returning to the house. He thought she disliked the rain. She hated bad weather.

She pawed at him again, and threw up her head and howled,

frustrated beyond measure by the unbelievable idiocy of the people around her.

'All right. Find, girl,' Dai said wearily. It was worth a chance, anything was worth a chance, but his feelings were bitter when, once more, she raced towards the house and howled outside the now closed back door.

CHAPTER SEVEN

NED FOLEY, huddled into his greatcoat, was aware of aching back and complaining legs, and weariness because he had not been near his bed all night. He stood pondering. He knew Mark better than any of them, perhaps better than his own father, who was always too busy and seldom had time for himself, let alone his family. Mark had undoubtedly gone after Elliott. The most likely place was in the big elm beyond the house. Ned looked up. Day was with them, a grey day, a dull day, a desolate day, the sky banked with clouds that poured their cargo over sodden land. Wind roared through the trees. The river flung itself headlong, hurling boulders that clapped together like thunder. Had Mark been in the elm, he would surely have fallen. Ned had looked on the ground beneath all the trees. There was no sign of the boy. The frenzied river roared beyond the wall. He shivered.

The tree bent its branches towards the roof. Ned glanced upwards. There was a gleam of colour beside the chimney stack. His eyes were old. He blinked, and turning, grabbed Sergeant Henty's arm as the policeman walked wearily through the yard, dreading the report he would have to make to Sheila. He eased his collar away from his neck. Damn the weather.

'Up there, on the roof, by the stack.'

Ned could scarcely articulate in his anxiety. The sergeant stared at the old man, wondering if he was out of his mind and then looked up. A moment later he raced across the yard, reaching the back door as Dai opened it to let Deedee inside.

'Damn' stupid dog,' Dai said furiously. 'All she can think of is getting out of the wet.'

'Oh no, it's not,' the sergeant said. 'Look, man. See where she's going.'

At last they were paying attention to her, and impatience sent the Great Dane flying ahead of them, eager to show them her discovery. She raced through the hall and up the stairs, barking. Tim ran after her, the sergeant at his heels, taking the stairs two at a time, while Dai followed, unaware of their goal, and sure they were all demented. Ned, step by slow, careful step, aching in every muscle, cursing his age, dragged behind. Nearly seventy and with too many creaks to show for it. Rheumatism plagued him. He thought it must be the result of nights spent in the open, of days soaked by rain, of constant exposure to bad weather. Once he would have been first up the stairs, and first to reach the lad. He'd never had wife nor chick of his own, but he liked kids and Mark was almost a grandson to him. Ned regretted his lack of family now that he was old.

Deedee flew into the attic, stood at the ladder's foot, and barked furiously. Mark heard her. His thin answering shout reached the man below. The sergeant climbed the ladder, thrust the skylight open, and looked up at the small, forlorn, huddled figure. Mark could not believe his eyes. Uncontrollable tears ran down his cheeks, infuriating him.

The sergeant inspected the roof. It was so steep that it was a death trap, and it was a miracle the kid hadn't fallen. Mark was wedged against the chimney stack and dared not move. He was so stiff that he thought his legs and arms would never work again. He was so cold that his teeth chattered violently. He was soaked to the skin, and so was Elliott, who had given up protesting and was huddled in damp misery inside Mark's shirt.

'Hey,' said a voice, below them.

It was Dave Hinney, brother to Rob Hinney, the cowman at Wellans, who had been searching with the other men, out on the fells, and heard the commotion from the kitchen as he drank coffee. Sheila kept the kettle boiling all night. Sleep was unthinkable.

'I've done some tiling. Let me get out there. I'm used to roofs.'

Dave climbed out of the skylight. He moved, catlike, towards the ridge, and bent to put his arm round Mark's shoulders.

'If I hang on to you, can you crawl towards the sergeant?' he asked.

Mark nodded, but almost screamed when he moved. Every muscle seemed to have seized, and to be protesting against a

52

change in posture. His feet were numb and cramps agonized both arms. He slipped, and Dave, balanced against the chimney, put both arms under Mark's armpits. The boy was a dead weight. The sergeant, standing on the ladder, reached up and took hold of him, and, with difficulty, helped him down the steep rungs and into the attic.

There was no time for recriminations. Mark could not stand. He slumped to the floor, totally exhausted.

'Exposure,' the sergeant said.

They knew all about that and what it did to men lost on the fells. It was a constant hazard, as much to be feared as a broken skull or a fractured limb.

Sheila was ready with rough towels and blankets. She stripped off the soaked clothes, and discovered the kitten, crouched, shivering, and stiff. Mollie, appearing suddenly, anxious-faced, having just come in from a futile, frightening search along the river bank, took Elliott down to dry and warm him, knowing the drill well. Animals often got into trouble in winter when snow masked the fells and drifted deep and the beasts were buried. Mollie set to work. She had phoned the stables earlier, and been given the day off, but the stables were understaffed. She would catch the ten o'clock bus, now Mark was found.

Ned could do little to help. He stumbled wearily downstairs, to telephone the doctor, told the waiting men that Mark was safe, though far from well, and poured coffee and handed round sandwiches that Sheila had busied herself making, unable to rest, unable to think, unable to relax. Relief lightened the searchers' moods, but no one had much to say, and Jo Needler voiced the opinion of them all.

'Bloody silly to think the poor kid was there under our noses all the time,' he said.

'We'd never've seen him, even if we'd looked up,' one of the policemen said. 'It was blacker than torment, all night.'

Dai carried his son down to his bedroom, wrapped him in more blankets, and laid him on the bed. Mark lay motionless. Exhaustion and exposure soon claimed victims. It needed so little time, out in the cold and the wind and the wet, before human resistance was put to strain. Dai remembered cadets, and scouts, and even grown men, who died after a night on the fells, and cursed the chance that sent the kitten through the hole in the roof. Ned, glad to find something to do, was mending it now, hammering another piece of wood over it, ensuring it was cat-proof. Kittens were always adventurous.

There was a great deal to be done. Dai had two cats to spay before morning surgery. He went upstairs to shave, and change, and then, half an hour later, went in to look at his son. He stood beside the bed. The boy was sleeping, his face white, bruised shadows under his eyes. Only Mark would have been caught out like that, he reflected. Susie always came to her father for help, and Mollie would never, even when younger, have attempted anything so foolhardy. Tim might have climbed after Elliott, but he would have wedged the trapdoor first. Mark's life was one long series of escapades.

Downstairs, Mollie prepared breakfast, and made her mother join her. Sheila sat, listless, picking at the food, forcing herself to eat. Coffee was welcome, warming her. She was chilled with fear. She had known too many cases of exposure to be complacent. Elliott, recovering, lay in front of the fire, and presently walked unsteadily towards the saucer of milk in the corner of the room, and lapped a little, and returned to sleep, totally exhausted. Tia curled beside him, and her soothing tongue sped his recovery. Sim had slipped quietly upstairs, always favouring Mark above any other member of the family, and was under the eiderdown, hidden from disapproving eyes.

Ned, the skylight safely covered, shared their meal. The other men had left, on their way to seek a shave and a change of clothing and go, sleepless, to their work.

'I'll help with the animals,' Ned said, knowing that there were many to feed and clean.

Sheila's morning round reminded her at times of the Zoo. Today it was more like slavery. Her eyes were gritty, her tongue was thick and furry, and her legs and arms seemed to disobey her will. She dropped a cup, as she was taking it to the sink. It broke, one more irritation in a day made up of irritations.

Ned, exploring, was trying to find out where all the animals slept, and which needed feeding. He opened the annexe door,

54

discovering the Persian cat and her kittens. The cat was hungry and jumped from her basket, weaving round the old man's legs. Animals always went to Ned immediately, sensing from his attitude that he could be trusted not to harm them.

He closed the door on the cat, and went to the kitchen to prepare her food. Sheila met him as he was carrying the plate to the annexe.

'That's a splendid animal,' he said.

Sheila looked at him miserably.

'She has to be spayed and the kittens put to sleep,' she said. 'Dai put it off. Susie knew about them. We'll have to try and hand-rear them. You know Susie.'

Ned nodded. Susie's blind love of every living creature was a constant headache.

He followed Sheila to the annexe. It had once been a conservatory but was now bare of plants. It was ideal for nursing families, as warm pipes regulated the temperature, a tiled floor ensured easy cleaning, and owing to the glass roof, the ventilation was excellent and draught free. There were two battered wicker chairs marked by generations of teeth and claws.

Tia and her kittens had lived here briefly, and Elliott had made full use of them, struggling up the legs at an age at which most kittens were far too timid to try such a venture.

Mollie was nearly ready to go to work. She looked into the annexe, her attitude warning Sheila of trouble.

'What is it?' she asked.

'Mrs. Hicks. She wants to know if Dad's spayed her cat and put . . .'

She stopped in dismay, as the old lady walked calmly past her, infuriating Sheila by her intrusion. Unfortunately, Mrs. Hicks was formidable, and Sheila was in no mood to deal with her. The old lady's husband had been a bishop, who died leaving his widow endowed with an arrogance that daunted everyone she met. She was tall, her white hair arranged in symmetrical waves, her black clothes imparting an air of perpetual mourning. Mollie fled.

'Why aren't those kittens dead, as I asked?'

There was no feeling in the old woman's voice. She looked down at the basket.

Sheila was overtired, she was desperately worried about Mark, she was overworked, she had had enough. She hated, above all things, putting down young animals.

'They're not dead because we aren't executioners,' she said, and listened to herself in sudden horror. 'My husband didn't train for five years in order to destroy animals for people who won't accept responsibility, or who keep pets for all the wrong reasons.'

Ned, appalled, tried to intervene, but Sheila could not be checked. She was tired of death; tired of stupid people, of impossible people, of selfish people, and of ignorant people, who inflicted more harm by indifference than was ever inflicted by cruelty.

'You had no right to have the cat if you weren't prepared to look after her. You could easily have had her spayed before she had kittens, if you didn't want her to have them. Why turn us into destroyers? You've no right . . . I sometimes think God was raving mad when he made people,' Sheila finished, and unexpectedly burst into tears.

Startled, Mrs. Hicks took the chair that Ned had vacated, and looked at Sheila helplessly.

'I didn't want the cat at all,' she said.

Sheila dried her eyes and sniffed.

'Then why did you have her?'

Mrs. Hicks was no longer arrogant.

'My sister died a month ago and left her to me in her will. I was very fond of Ellen, and she thought so highly of her Persian. She knew I never liked animals, and cats in particular, but she was so besotted she was sure I would overcome my dislike. It was even worse when I realized the creature was going to have kittens. I thought I might manage to tolerate her if she was spayed. She can live in the kitchen and not come near me. I can feed her. And see she is well, and comfortably housed.'

'That's no way to keep a cat, ma'am,' Ned said. 'It needs affection. Now look, you let me have her. My old fellow was put to sleep a few days ago and I haven't replaced him yet. She'll have a good home with me.'

'Would you really take her?' Mrs. Hicks' voice had come to life.

Ned nodded emphatically.

'I'll take her, kittens and all, if you're sure you don't want her back.'

He bent to stroke the Persian and she rubbed her head against his hand.

'I didn't even know Sukie could be affectionate,' the old lady said.

She stood up, and Sheila no longer found her formidable, but diminished, a woman caught by circumstance, trying, to the best of her limited ability, to perform a task for which she had no liking. Mrs. Hicks hesitated.

'I'm very glad your son is safe,' she said, and walked out, leaving Sheila staring at Ned, blinking away tears.

'Oh lord, Ned,' she said, 'what on earth possessed me? You won't tell Dai?'

Ned grinned his gap-toothed grin, and his blue eyes were friendly.

'It's had its effect,' he said. Sheila looked up at him ruefully.

'People,' she said, 'I often think I prefer animals, and then, quite suddenly something happens, and you feel maybe humans aren't so bad after all.'

The black Persian stretched herself, and walked delicately round the conservatory. Ned picked up his coffee cup, and sat down again in the chair. The day had lost all urgency. There was plenty to do at the House of Beasts. He sat, warmed by company, and Sukie jumped on his knee, and kneaded his trouser leg, purring. Ned rubbed her beneath her chin. The purrs increased, ecstatic. She was totally content, and Sheila smiled, knowing that the cat would have a good home, and the affection she craved. Ned was no sentimentalist, but he knew how to care for animals. There were few men like him. Tramp, poacher, rogue, people said, but she'd trust him with her children, her animals, her life.

CHAPTER EIGHT

IT was a grim-faced Ned who faced Dai a few weeks later, half an hour after morning surgery had ended. Life was unusually quiet; no epidemics and no emergencies. Mark had recovered and gone back to school. Even the kennels was almost empty, its only inmate a bitch in season, sent by her owners to board till her heat was ended as she was too young for pups, and at home she lived with two dogs. She was a gentle creature, a red setter, rangy with youth, her coat sleek and gloriously coloured.

Her bark, greeting Ned, was Dai's first intimation of unexpected work. He went to the door, and called, but the old man had no cheery reply. He plodded on, his face bleak, his eyes angry. He was carrying a dog in his arms.

'Here,' he said, offering the dog to Dai, 'and for God's sake don't speak to me for a few minutes, or happen I'll say things that shouldn't be said in a place where children might hear.'

Dai took the dog, shocked. There was a long weal across his shoulders, where the hair had been scorched away. It looked as if a red-hot poker had been laid across the animal's back. One leg dangled uselessly. Dai carried him into the surgery and laid him on the table. Terrified brown eyes stared up at the vet. The animal attempted a snarl, but was too weak to do more than lift his lips away from his teeth.

Dai's gentle hands explored the damaged body. He judged that the animal, a young and well-bred Alsation, was ten months old. The sable and chestnut coat was harsh with neglect. Ribs showed stark, thinly covered by flesh, and both eyes were sore and running.

Dai didn't know where to start. He needed time to think and began to bathe the sore eyes. The dog made no protest. He watched every movement. His ears moved as the vet spoke gently, relying on his voice to soothe away fear.

Ned, at the window, was looking out into a garden that had not yet given itself to winter's grip. Although it was November, a clematis flower decorated the vine by the front door, and roses were blooming in the bed beyond the gravelled drive.

'People!' Ned said bitterly.

'Where did he come from, Ned?' Dai asked, anger sharpening his voice. The leg was badly broken in two places. The dog was a mess. He began to cut fur away from the burn, and as he did so, sickness gathered and fury grew, until he did not know how to hold it in check. He patted the Alsatian, and went to stand beside Ned at the window. He was shaking with temper.

'Well?' Dai asked. 'That burn's deep and it's septic. I've never seen such a thing. Who owns him?'

'If you can make a case stick, I'm a witness,' Ned said, 'and by God, if I can make the brute suffer, I will. Mrs. Jones and I were chatting, on the corner by the new by-pass, when this car came along, going like a running fox with hounds at his throat. He must have been doing near forty-five when he opened the door and shoved the dog out. I got his number. He couldn't have seen us. We were tucked behind the wall out of the wind. He'd never have dared if he'd known there were folk about.' The dog was watching them, its eyes forlorn.

'I wish to God people would think twice before they buy a pup!' Daid said bitterly. He went back to do what he could. The poor beast lay patient, and licked Ned's hand as he came over to stroke its head.

'Call us a civilized nation.' The old man looked sick. 'I feel like doing murder.'

Dai's brown face creased in a rueful grin.

'Justifiable homicide. I know how you feel,' he said. It was hard to hold his own fury in check. He stroked the dog gently. 'I've no choice but to put him down. Nobody's going to nurse him – and heaven only knows what his temper will be like after this lot.'

'I'll take him,' Ned said. 'Always did like a challenge. Remember that fox we found, with her foot half chewed off when she was caught in a trap? We fixed her up, you and me. And she lived to run free again. It ought to be easier to fix up a dog. This one's never had a chance, poor brute. He might as

59

well find out there is some fun in life. He's not beyond help, is he?'

Dai shook his head. Sheila, who had just come home in the estate wagon, saw the two men at the open window, and came towards them.

'Trouble?' she asked.

Dai nodded, and she hurried inside, and looked at the dog.

'Oh, Dai,' she said, helplessly. The burn, now free of fur, was a gape of yellow pus.

'It's a miracle he survived at all,' Dai said, thinking of the speed of the car.

'It's a miracle that'd better not be spoiled,' Ned said. 'That's my dog now, and you get him right for me, Dai Evans.'

He nodded to Sheila, and walked to the door.

'Stay for lunch, Ned,' Sheila said. 'There's only the two of us, with the children at school. And if you've time, you can clean Dai's Land-Rover. It looks as if it's been sitting in a farmyard for weeks, being used as a roost by the hens.'

By the time the children came home to tea the Alsatian was recovering from the anaesthetic. His leg had been pinned and plastered, and the burn cleaned. Dai put the dog in a big basket in a corner of the study near the fire. He took his accounts and papers, and worked at his desk, ready to comfort the animal, should he show signs of distress. The vet had been working for over an hour before he felt eyes watching him. The dog was wide awake, lying quietly, without complaint. In all its short life the Alsatian had never known a moment free from fear of some form of physical attack from the family with whom it lived. The man kicked it. His wife, afraid, hit it frequently with its lead. The burn had been inflicted by the elder son, a fifteen-year-old bully who also terrorized his younger brother, and half the neighbourhood children. Here, in the quiet room, was incredible peace. Dai walked over to the basket and knelt beside it.

'Good dog,' he said, knowing the tone of his voice would be reassurance, even if the animal had never been taught to understand words.

The long tail wagged briefly, a feeble twitch that was its own reward. Ned, coming into the room with two glasses of beer, looked down, his expression lightening.

'He's a nice brute,' he said abruptly. 'I wonder if he'll settle with me?'

Ned had left the door open. Elliott, anxious to find company and warmth by the fire, slipped quietly into the room. Perennially curious, the kitten walked over to look at the Alsatian. The dog moved one ear. A moment later Elliott jumped into the basket and began to lick the dog's injured side. The Alsatian sighed deeply. Elliott settled to sleep.

Dai went out, to look at a mare due to foal, at a farm further down the valley. He returned, over an hour later, to find Ned sitting beside the Alsatian, talking, while the brown eyes and gently moving ears showed that the dog was listening intently.

'I'll keep an eye on him,' Ned said. 'He might feel bad in the night, or want to go outside. I'd like to start him off well, and let him get to know me.'

Ned was a godsend, Dai reflected, as he went to the kitchen where Sheila was making coffee, and the Great Dane was begging for a walk.

Sheila fetched her coat, and Deedee stretched herself and followed her mistress, walking sedately, her elegant body panther-like as she passed through the shadows.

Sheila stood at the gate, and looked at the night. Frost tinged the air, and a faint rime shone on the hedges. She turned and looked towards the fells, where dusk hid fox and weasel, and hunting stoat. An owl flew low and Deedee stared up at it, moonlight reflecting from her eyes.

Beyond the darkness Horton Lake mirrored the sky, its surface gleaming cold. Sheila looked at the lamplight that marked each farm, glancing across to Sheerlings, which was centuries old, haunted by the past, and now threatened by the present. There were several ghosts at Sheerlings, quiet appearances that troubled nobody. Sheila thought of water flooding the valley, of houses darkened forever, and shivered, unable to bear the thought. It was pitiless, destroying hopes. She looked into the distance, wishing she could remodel the whole world.

Far beyond Sheerlings were the lights of Deep Willows, once the scene of a violent battle between cavalier and roundhead, and here, too, at midnight, in the oak-beamed and -panelled dining-room, it was said that the place echoed to the sound of clashing swords. History had been made at every farmhouse on the fells. The Swan itself was an historic place, where Cromwell spent several days. A glimmer of an idea came into Sheila's head. Perhaps she had a weapon with which to fight the planners after all. She would have to find out, and until then she would keep her idea to herself. She did not wish to raise false hopes but she would have to act fast.

Dai had called in at Deep Willows two days before, to look at an ailing calf. He found Steve sunk in a depression so deep that his wife feared it was more than temporary. The farmer sat, taking no interest in his beasts, and when Lysbeth tried to rouse him, he raged at her, saying that life was not worthwhile. Why work at all when the place was going to be sunk under millions of gallons of water? What point in mending the roof or strengthening the byre, or in adding to the herd?

Lysbeth rarely gave way to her feelings, but Dai stood miserably in the cow byre, trying to find his handkerchief to stem her streaming tears. He came home morose and swore at Sheila, who only discovered the cause of his anger when they were in bed.

He sat, arms round his knees, fulminating and furious.

'We're all so bloody helpless,' he said, finally, as he turned off the light, and they lay silent, dreading the future. When, at last, sleep came, Sheila dreamed of floods, and herself marooned, and Deedee barking. She woke suddenly to find that the Great Dane really was barking and she had overslept.

Now, standing at the gate, the memory of her dream returned. She looked over the fells, while Deedee waited patiently. A moment later, the Great Dane stiffened, growling softly. Sheila turned her head as a dog fox loped by, his brush streaming behind him. He paused, and looked at her, before he went on his way. Her hand dropped to the Great Dane's collar, feeling excitement thrill the animal. Sheila wondered why Deedee accepted Rusty, and yet quivered at strange foxes. The fox vanished, silent as nightfall.

The lights went out on the fells. Sheerling lay dark, its bulk invisible; Deep Willows vanished in gloom; the street lamps dimmed and died; the Swan, last of all to sleep, merged into the night. Nothing was left but the wind keening softly over the dusty heather, and the memory of man.

Perhaps in a few years, nothing else would be left. Only the wide stretch of water, a few birds wading, and under the water the ruins of many hopes.

Above her the stars shone, remote points of light, in an infinite and scarcely comprehensible universe. Looking up, she wondered if the creatures on the world were of any importance; or if, in millennia to come, all of them, including man, would be nothing more than a teasing memory in a chain of unforeseeable events.

Such thoughts brought despair. The dog beside her, the moon above her, the house behind her, these were reality. Footsteps echoed on the drive. Dai came towards her, and stood beside her, looking over the valley, not needing to ask her thoughts. Together, they turned and walked towards the House of Beasts.

Sheila went to bed. Dai went to his study and looked at the Alsatian. Mark had come downstairs and was talking to Ned.

'I couldn't sleep,' he said, as his father raised an eyebrow. 'I feel sick.'

'You ate enough for three at supper, so I'm not surprised,' Dai said unsympathetically. He went to the kitchen and came back with a glass of his own indigestion mixture.

'Next time, I'll give you what I give a greedy cow,' he threatened. 'That would make you think. Back to bed, now.'

Mark took the glass and hurried back to his room.

'Mark's sobered down since his night on the tiles,' Ned said, grinning.

'I think it did him good because it was so damned silly,' Dai said. 'Stuck outside on the roof of your own home, unable to make anyone hear, while half the village lose a night's sleep hunting for you, and you watch.'

'He had a nasty do afterwards, for all that,' said Ned. Mark had been ill for several days, and off school for over a week.

'If it only teaches him sense, it'll have been worth it,' Dai said sombrely. 'I've always had visions of Mark killing himself in some harebrained adventure. I dread the day when he's old enough to drive.'

Ned, left alone with the dog, sat looking at the fire, thinking of other dogs and other days, when he had been spry enough to lead the Hunt, and walked miles over the fells. Times changed, but people didn't change. They were still as stupid as they ever were, and in many ways as cruel, without even meaning the cruelty half the time. And half the time they did. Man was a nasty little animal at his worst. And the world didn't seem to get any better.

He sighed, and the dog struggled out of his basket and rested his head on Ned's foot, knowing, for the first time in a miserable and confused existence, that here was a human he could trust.

Flames leapt in the chimney. The clock whirred and struck midnight. An owl called in the garden. Ned dozed, wishing that life was less dull, and age less of a penance, quite unaware that the dog at his feet was going to give him a new interest, which would lead him into unexpected byways.

CHAPTER NINE

IT was almost Christmas before the Alsatian was fit. Susie christened him Sable. Ned, taking him home as soon as he was able to hop on three legs, found the animal gentle and affectionate. Sable had never known kindness before, and rewarded Ned with unstinting loyalty. He had had little training. He was meticulously clean, but that was all.

The burn healed, and new fur grew over the scar. The leg, which had broken in two places, was a slower job, and Dai thought the dog might well be lame for the rest of his life.

Sable was used to cats, and jealousy was unknown to him. He made friends with Sukie, the black Persian, sleeping beside her at night on the rag rug that Bess Logan had pegged, in front of the dying fire. The kittens were gone, except for Soot, a small bouncy tom, who thought that Sable's sole purpose in life was to amuse him. Sukie washed Sable whenever she groomed Soot. Ned, amused by the animals, called them his three S's, and was even more amused when the Alsatian started to wash the kitten too. Poor Soot existed in a state of permanent dampness.

As the dog recovered his confidence, he began to play. Running, at first, was difficult, but he could lie and pat at the kitten, who pawed back, stalked Sable's tail, clambered fearlessly all over the Alsatian, and frequently settled to sleep between the dog's front paws.

Ned discovered that Sable learned quickly, and loved to obey. He learned the meaning of 'no' so easily that Ned was able to stop him worrying at the plaster after only two days, during both of which he had done his best to remove the annoying cast. He hated it, but he left it alone.

As soon as the plaster was removed, Ned taught the dog to come to his name, and taught him his manners. Dai, passing one day during lessons, watched with interest.

'I wish you'd show some of the villagers how to train their dogs, Ned,' he said, half joking.

Ned stared at the vet. It was an idea. It was more than an idea. It was a brainwave, and what's more, he'd have a go at some of the Shows with Sable. The dog had it born in him to work, and it would provide fascinating occupation for both of them. He'd always been interested in handling dogs, but never owned a pedigree animal before.

The police had made inquiries about the Alsatian. Prosecution was pending. Meanwhile Ned could keep the dog. The owners willingly surrendered the pedigree form, hoping compliance would soften the heart of the law. Sable had an impressive ancestry. Ned was more than ever convinced that many people were mad. They had paid a small fortune for the dog, and now they did not want it.

By the end of the week, he had infected Sheila with his enthusiasm, and, each weekday, when lunch was over and the house was quiet, Ned brought Sable and Sheila called Deedee, and they began a training session. Ned was sure that if they produced results they could interest the villagers in a Dog Obedience Club. Dai, seeing possibilities in the plan, encouraged it with all his will. If he could get enough owners together he could impress on them the need for the inoculation to prevent distemper, for proper feeding, to prevent obesity; and for training to make their pets biddable and reasonable creatures to have around. All his own were taught to obey simple commands but none of them had been trained any further. It would be interesting to see how Ned and Sheila progressed.

The children were busy with Christmas. Mollie made her own presents, and spent much of her time at home shut up in her bedroom, with a notice on the door saying 'Do Not Disturb'. Tim was doing odd jobs for the villagers, to earn enough money to buy his. He exercised three dogs and one horse, cleaned four cars, and on Saturdays, helped at the village shop, delivering grocery orders.

Mark had forgotten to save any of his pocket money. He was always generous, buying Susie a paperback book that she particularly wanted, or buying his mother fresh farm eggs on his way home from school.

Unable to think of any way of buying presents, he suggested extra pocket money, causing his father's right eyebrow to achieve such a startling elevation that he changed his mind, and went to try and cajole his mother. Sheila, knowing the choice lay between paying for help, or lending him money, offered a small wage for cleaning the kennels. Mark looked at her in dismay, but dared not argue. Sheila smiled at his retreating back. She knew that in spite of his distaste, Mark would do his best.

Susie had saved fifty pence, and was waiting to be taken to shop. Sheila dreaded the excursion, as Susie was a careful shopper, who hunted diligently until she found exactly what she wanted, and could afford. She made an exceedingly ambitious list and showed it to Dai, who, managing a rare uninterrupted evening at the beginning of December, helped her plan more sensibly.

Dai suggested pencils for Mollie, Tim, and Mark, and two cubes of bath salts for Sheila. Sheila suggested a little reminder pad and pencil for the surgery for Dai. Susie could make the pad herself, and buy the pencil. The child was busy, her tongue in her cheek, an expression of intense concentration on her face, cutting irregular pieces of paper to more or less the same size, when the snow began.

Snow was fun. She watched from the window, as it fell in huge flakes from a lowering, leaden sky. It would soon be night. Mark was cleaning the kennels. Mollie, home unusually early for once, was helping Sheila. Tim had a biology examination in the morning. He was sitting over his books, deaf and blind to everything around him.

Tia came to sit by Susie and stare at the snow. She pressed her nose against the window, watching the falling flakes drift enticingly. She patted at them with her paws, a dancing, elegant, quicksilver sprite, beautiful as a ballerina.

Dai poured himself a cup of tea and ate a crispbread, wishing Sheila was more lenient over his diet. He stood beside the window, his thoughts very different from his small daughter's. The snow was early. It had not been forecast, and sudden snow on the fells often meant disaster. The far-ranging sheep were easily trapped. He wondered how many of the farms had brought the sheep close to the house. There would be flooding too, later, if the snow lay deep, and the thought reminded him of the scheme to inundate the valley. The village had produced a petition. Steve Johns and Ted Wellans had both briefed their solicitors, the Vicar had written to their Member of Parliament, and there was to be a hearing after Christmas. The thought depressed him. So much depended on the outcome. More farms and cottages were affected than he had imagined possible.

Sheila, busy with Christmas preparations, seemed also to have embarked on a course of study. There were library books everywhere, many of them historical, and, whatever she was planning, she did not confide in her husband. Dai wondered if it was anything to do with Christmas, or if she had suddenly decided to write a book. He tied a knot in his handkerchief to remind himself to buy a present for his wife, and asked the children if she had voiced any wishes. Tim suggested a dishwasher, which was out of the question. Mark had no ideas. Mollie, vague and unhelpful, said, 'something pretty', and Susie, predictably, said 'a St. Bernard puppy. Mummy always wanted a St. Bernard.'

Snow fell all night, disguising the familiar world, so that they woke to a glitter of glory, dazzling under a brilliant sun. Dai went out to feed the animals, locked up safely, in barn and coachhouse, in the annexe and the study. Tia rubbed herself against his legs. Sim ran into the kitchen looking for food, and helped Dai find the spade to dig a path across the yard, weaving hungrily around his legs. There was no school. The House of Beasts was often temporarily isolated by snow, worrying Dai, who hoped no animal would need him desperately. Beyond the hedge, the plough was clearing the road. Mollie could not get to the stables, and began to help her mother.

Sim grumbled, his miaows irritating. He was cold. Susie came downstairs in jersey and jeans and anorak, anxious to go out of doors, and run in the garden and build a snowman. Conker called to her from his stall, his amiable face watching for visitors. He was a friendly, pleasant-tempered horse. Susie brought him an apple, and gave him a hug, before running back to play. If only the snow would last forever. It would be fun not to have any more school.

An hour later, Tia and Sim and the dogs had been fed. Tim,

vaguely counting heads, looked all over the house, and then came into the kitchen, anxious.

'Where's Elliott?'

Elliott was nowhere. They searched every room again, calling. Tia and Sim searched too. Deedee joined in, hopefully, expecting the little cat to leap out at her, but Elliott was not behind the furniture, or under it. He was not in any of the drawers, and he had not crawled into a cupboard. Tim searched the attics.

Dai searched the annexe and surgery and study, and Mark and Mollie searched the rooms.

'He must be outside,' Susie said. 'He'll be buried, and he'll die.'

Her voice rose to a wail, and tears spilled over. Mollie hastened to comfort her, and Dai called Deedee and went into the garden. Deedee was never very good at tracking in snow.

By teatime Susie was so distressed that she was put to bed, while Mollie sat beside her, reading, to distract her. There was no sign of Elliott. The sky threatened them, brooding sullen and yellow over undulating fells, where all familiar landmarks were hidden.

The snowplough cleared the village street. Ned brought Sable out for exercise. The dog had never seen snow before, and played the fool, jumping into it, until he terrified himself by vanishing into a drift, so that Ned had to dig frantically and haul on the Alsatian's hind legs. Sable was much more careful after that, and stayed so close at heel that Ned almost fell over him.

The old man appeared at the back door of the House of Beasts, stamping snow from his feet.

'You all look glummer than last year's bad deeds,' he said.

'We can't find Elliott,' Mark said miserably. 'And you know Susie.'

'He's outside somewhere, buried under the snow,' Tim said.

That was now a certainty.

Ned looked at the hidden garden. There was almost an acre of ground, and search was impossible. Sable was running without a trace of lameness, and Deedee had joined him, chasing, crazy, winter mad. Their paws left giant skidmarks through which the green grass showed, scarlike.

'It's not much use trying to find him,' Dai said. 'Where would we begin?'

Nobody knew. Sheila went indoors. Susie would have to face this and learn that accidents happened, no matter how careful you were. Elliott was so small he could slip through a door when someone else opened it, and remain unnoticed. Poor Elliott. He hated cold, and he hated being alone. And, judging by the chill in the air, a hard frost was due that night. At least that meant no more snow. It seldom lasted long at this time of year. The real trouble came later. She always dreaded the first months of the New Year.

Deedee had given up her game. She was stately and feeling her age, and the Alsatian was a frisky nuisance.

He barked, teasing her, but she stalked indoors, disdainful.

Sable wanted to run. He chased round the garden, jumping where the snow was deep, scuffing it with his nose, scattering it with his paws. Ned left him outside, knowing that even if the dog did fall into a drift they could easily track him. The gate was closed and he could not jump over the wall. It was far too high. He went into the kitchen, where the fire glowed brightly, and the children's evening meal was laid on a gay scarlet seersucker cloth, which covered the big scrubbed whitewood table. Sheila poured a cup of tea, and Ned went back to the window. The Alsatian was amusing himself by hunting through the snow, digging at intervals as if his life depended on it.

He barked.

Ned ran outside as fast as his old legs would take him. Sable never made an unnecessary noise. Dai and the boys followed and found the dog digging frantically. Snow flew behind the busy paws. Tim began to dig too, using his hands as scoops. A few minutes later, they cleared the ground, and there, in a deep hollow, was Elliott. He moved feebly, and yowled to them. Dai picked him up, pushing the little cat inside his coat, and hurried to the house, while Ned stopped to reward his dog with pats and a romp and well-deserved praise.

Susie and Mollie had come down to the kitchen. Susie held tightly to her sister's hand, as Dai rubbed Elliott gently with a warm towel. Tia and Sim jumped up and began to use their tongues. Nobody moved or spoke.

When Elliott opened his eyes and flicked an ear, Dai put him in Tia's basket. Sim and Tia jumped down to welcome him back. Susie raced at her father and hugged him hard.

'I'm so glad you're a vet,' she announced.

Tension broke and everyone laughed.

'Well I am.'

Susie flushed indignantly, and bent to stroke Elliott, who purred softly, and licked her hand, delighted to be noticed, and now comfortably warm.

CHAPTER TEN

THE snow vanished as swiftly as it had come, much to Dai's relief, and his family gave themselves completely to excitement.

There were always three Christmas trees at the House of Beasts, although there was seldom time to celebrate. Animals, like children, were unaware that this was an inconvenient time to be ill. Dai expected casualties, although he always hoped that, just this once, nothing untowards might occur.

At Christmas he longed, more than ever, for a partner, and drafted yet another advertisement for the columns of the professional journals. He rarely received replies. There was no dearth of work for qualified men, and his far-flung practice was unattractive.

Dai, standing at the window, looked out on a grey day in late December. Christmas was nudging, goading the most Scrooge-like into making lists and buying cards. The postman called three times a day, and soon students, home from college, would be helping out. Susie was busy with her tree, which was outside the waiting-room door. No one could remember how the custom started, but now, every year, Tim decked the little fir with coloured lights, and Susie hung titbits for the birds from its branches.

She threaded peanuts on string, and hung up half-coconuts filled with seed, and lumps of fat pierced by skewers were hammered into the trunk. For the next few weeks, the tree would be a rendezvous for every bird in the district, and at night, when the coloured lamps glowed warm, the boughs would be alive with little creatures huddled together, savouring the rare pleasure of roosting cosily, protected from the wintry cold, while the air was enlivened by their voices.

Susie's cheeks glowed red as her anorak, and she was so engrossed that she did not see her father watching her. He had finished surgery and his only call that day was to Steve Johns' farm, where two calves were ailing.

Tia and Sim sat side by side, their eyes following Susie's movements. Sim watched unmoved, but Tia was entranced, and prowled and grabbed at the dangling strings. Elliott, arriving, as usual, full-pelt, raced up the trunk and tapped Susie's hand. Irritated, she lifted him down. He ran up again and knocked down the half-coconut that she had tied a moment before. Dai laughed, and went to find his wife.

Sheila's head was filled with thoughts of food. Both Rusty and Deedee watched her, eyes eager, expectant. The kitchen was filled with savoury smells. She always prepared a splendid Christmas dinner, although it was three years since Dai had been able to join them. There were always emergencies. The first year a guard dog at a factory had been attacked, and brutally injured, by a man who broke in, and Dai drove over to put the animal to sleep. Next year he had been out all day with a calving cow, and last year there had been an exceedingly nasty accident that effectively ruined Christmas for all of them. A neighbour's child, riding a new pony, had been thrown. The pony bolted across fields on to the motorway, being hit by a car, whose occupants were badly injured. The child herself was badly hurt, and the pony beyond recovery.

If only he could get through this Christmas without disasters. He left Sheila grappling with her grocery list and went into the cold. The wind snatched at his throat. He stopped for a word with Susie, and invited Deedee into the Land-Rover. It was a rare treat, and she jumped in joyfully. He patted her head. He would not be long at Deep Willows, and it was good to have company on his drive, even if it were only the dog's.

Lysbeth met him at the gate.

'I can't get any sense out of Steve,' she said.

She looked across the yard, noting the endless waiting jobs. She was doing most of the work herself, as one of the men was ill. Steve scarcely roused himself to take any interest in the farm.

'What's the use?' was all he would say. He stared out of the window, seeing, not the well-run acres, but enclosing floods, and the unceasing sound of water roared in his ears.

'He won't go to the doctor, or let him come here. I asked him to look in, but Steve locked himself in his office and wouldn't come out. He says nothing's the matter.

Lysbeth's eyes were bleak. There was little Dai could do, and no comfort he could offer. He examined the calves and injected them. He went in to talk to Steve but received no answer. His thoughts were dismal as he negotiated the twisting moorland road. If only Steve had reacted like Ted Wellans, who, goaded to frenzied activity, was tilting at windmills, writing letters to the press, stirring up his solicitor, who was sure he would go mad, as Ted had no idea of the lengthy procedures necessary in law, and wanted instant results. Ted tried to involve Steve, but Steve accepted defeat without lifting a finger. Lysbeth might have battled, but with all the responsibility of the farm, she was weary. She watched Dai drive away. Christmas would be a mockery this year.

Christmas Eve was wet, a swine of a day, rain lashing from a dull sky that brooded over the hills, merging with Hortonmere, and soaking everyone who had occasion to go out of doors. Dai, returning from a follow-up visit to Deep Willows, had a headache, and a sore throat, and a temper fit for a king. Half the village had flu. He hated his job. He hated being unable to help a sick beast, beyond prescribing for it.

Dusk was approaching, earlier than ever. The lights of the village houses were warm and welcoming, and he was alone in the cold. Brilliant baubles glittered on the Christmas tree outside the church, and three small children stood looking up at it, hand in hand, entranced, as if heaven had manifested itself in glory, especially for them. There was a tiny tree in almost every window. The lights outside his waiting-room door could be seen as the Land-Rover turned the bend and began to climb the hill.

The house was brooding with excitement when he went inside, warmth almost taking his breath away. All three trees were decorated; outside, the lights gleamed a welcome; inside, in the waiting-room, stood another tree, high on a cupboard, evocative of many Christmases. The kitchen tree was also on a high cupboard, protected from the cats. Elliott had already broken three of the swinging baubles.

Sheila had been baking. Trays of mince pies stood on the dresser, and Susie was icing the cake, intense concentration on her face. Rusty pressed against her leg, his fox face blissful. Elliott, watching the intriguing swirls, put out a paw that Susie slapped smartly, so that the little cat retreated, indignant tail swishing, and curled up with his back to the room, to show his extreme displeasure. He licked savagely at one of his white socks.

Dai had just poured himself a cup of tea when the telephone rang. Mark answered it. A moment later he handed it to his father, frowning.

'Some man wants you. He's a foreigner, Dad, and I can't understand him.'

The soft voice had an unidentifiable accent, and spoke a curious form of English. Dai frowned too, trying to catch the words. The line was faint and very bad.

'I am lone . . . the headman has flu . . . the owner is not here . . . our vet has flu, and says to call you. Please come . . . I think the mare will die. I can not help her.'

Dai wrote down the address. It was a stables nearly thirty miles away, not on his books, but if Dougal had flu there was nothing for it. He rang through to Dougal's home, and spoke to the other vet's wife. No chance of any help there. Dougal's temperature was over a hundred and one, and he should have packed up days before. And his wife would not let him even answer the phone. He sent a message to say the mare was highly temperamental and extremely valuable. It was not much help. Dai rang off. He drank his tea, took four of the mince pies, and went out again into the dark.

'A long job?' Sheila asked.

He looked back from the open door. The three cats were curled on the rug and Deedee was stretched full length, ecstatic, her belly exposed to the fire's warm blaze. Rusty lay beside her, his paw across her tail.

'A long job,' he said. He looked at the animals. 'Believe me, it's not the dogs that lead a dog's life!'

The door slammed behind him. Cold air hit him. Below him lights were strung along the street, and the Christmas tree outside the church shone bravely in the rain. Beyond his garden, carol singers sang, voices lifted joyously.

'Good Christian men rejoi-oi-oice,
With heart and soul and voi-oi-oice,
Give ye heed to what we say . ॥ ॥'

Dai let in the clutch and the roar of the Land-Rover engine drowned the words. Behind him, the house lights died away, and then he was in the village, and through the village street, and there was no more light. The dark fells stretched for miles, and he was alone in the wind and the rain, while the rest of the world celebrated.

He drove on, aware of the wind that flung itself across the dead heather; of an owl that flashed briefly in his headlights and was gone; of the endless twisting road that rose to the hairpin bend and dropped again to the rolling moorland. On a far hilltop a light flared, and he wondered. There, long ago, the Roman legions had waited, while the little wild men made constant war. What was up there on this Christmas Eve without one single star to show its promise? He shivered. He was tired, he felt ill, and he wished he were a child again, and could sleep safe in bed, with his mother to look after him. He must be going mental.

He slowed to avoid a straying sheep, and then there was nothing except the darkling fells, and the endless road, and the wind that hurled the rain against his windscreen, and twisted the wheel in his hands.

CHAPTER ELEVEN

THE stables, a large place, loose boxes grouped round three sides of a well-paved yard, stood at the edge of the little town of Trapperton. Rails bordered the paddocks, reflecting white from Dai's headlamps as he turned into the drive. Behind the stables, at a distance from them, lying black and bulky against the night, was a long low house. Blind windows stared at him.

Dai stopped the Land-Rover, climbing out stiffly, to be greeted by a stableman who came to meet him from one of the far blocks.

'I am Kurt Schwarz,' he said.

Dai found himself facing a thin elderly man, his face worn with years, his grey eyes tired, their expression sombre. His mouth was firm, beautifully shaped and surprisingly gentle, red against the thin white moustache that bordered his upper lip. His white hair, thick and wiry, was cut close to his head. He moved like a shadow, dapper in boots, breeches, and a spotless white shirt.

'I am sorry, Mr. Evans,' he said, in the soft unidentifiable accented voice. 'The mare does not know it is Christmas. I am so worried. She is not our mare. That makes it worse.'

He led the way to the foaling block and Dai looked about him, trying to remember all he had heard about the stables. Their stallion, Beowulf, was splendid, and mares from all over the country were sent to him, ready to foal when they arrived, and visit him when their foals were ten days old. The stable had bred several winners, and also, Dai knew, had a reputation for employing some of the best men in the world. The owner paid well, expected total loyalty and received it.

The foaling block contained two large apartments for the mares, with an office between for the groom. Kurt led Dai into a pleasantly furnished room, where a deep, chintz-covered arm-chair bulked large in front of the hearth. There was a big desk, a cupboard for instruments, a filing cabinet full of details of mares and their foals, and an electric fire that glowed brightly, mock flames dancing behind a glass panel.

'The mare is in here,' Kurt said, opening the door. 'Luckily she is the only one to foal tonight. The foal is more than ten days too early. It is a good job they sent her before Christmas. I do not like to leave her. She has been restless for so long. For longer than I ever know. It is her first foal and she is very frightened. And I am on my own. Everyone else have flu. We are short staffed also because it is Christmas.'

He opened the door and Dai, looking at the mare, knew that he was looking at a queen among horses. Even with the foal inside her, even in the throes of her birth pangs, the regal line of her neck and head, and the flow of her mane and tail, were splendid. Her great brown eyes stared at him, beseeching, unable to understand what racked her. Kurt moved unhurriedly to her head, murmuring softly.

'Ach, meine Kleine. Stay still, Liebling. Nah, nah, still, still.'

He stroked her neck, and patted her gently, before taking wisped straw to wipe sweat from her flanks. Dai went forward to examine her, hissing softly under his breath, reassuring her with his quietness, moving slowly, always watchful. Her fright-ened eyes, and her ears, which moved when he moved, were telltales of her state of mind. She plunged suddenly.

'Ach, be still, little one. Kurt will not let you harm. Hush now, Liebling.'

The words were meant to soothe her, were meaningless murmurs, and were succeeding in their intent. Dai, examining the mare, could not, at first, make out what was wrong. Something was. Far away, the bells of Christmas were ringing a peal. It wouldn't be the first time he had spent Christmas in a stable and it wouldn't be the last. He grunted wryly. He was never a man for symbolism. He spent hours at a time, at all times of the year, in stables. Another foal, another job. And another Christmas that was not a celebration. All in the day's work. There was a knife inside his skull, behind his eyes, twisting into his brain. He forced himself to concentrate.

78

Within ten minutes he was functioning again, forgetting that he was tired, and that his throat and head ached, that life, a few hours before, had seemed futile, and that he had wished he belonged to a different profession. Now he had a challenge in front of him, a challenge that had to be met. This, too, was another man's territory and he could not let Dougal down, not even though Dougal himself might be unable to perform what was beginning to look like a miracle.

'Is not good?' Kurt said, his eyes watching Dai.

The man moved swiftly as the mare dropped to the straw, aiming a frantic kick at her own belly. The muscle contractions were constant, at regularly spaced intervals, although still far apart, and the animal's face was agonized. Her breath quickened with each pain. Dai examined her, and then leaned against the wall, watching. He knew now what was wrong. He would have to manipulate the foal, and he wished it were not necessary. He was thankful he had had practice with Joe Elliott's mare.

'The foal's lying with one leg curled under. I'll have to try and straighten it,' he said.

Perhaps he could ease the leg and bring it into the correct position. The foal was small. Dai scrubbed his hands before smothering them afresh with antiseptic lubricant. The mare was on her feet again, her head turned, bewildered eyes staring at her distended body as if unable to believe that it was behaving so strangely, possessed by mysterious forces which had no part in her.

The clock ticked on the study wall. The wind whispered in the straw that lay loose in the yard, and both sounds highlighted the panting breaths of the distressed mare. Far away, church bells were pealing, a carillon from another time, another place, another world.

'Hush, hush, Liebling,' Kurt said, his hands soothing, gentling, and the mare rested her head against his cheek, needing comfort. She was alone among strangers, away from home, and she had never known such pain before. She swished her tail, flicking Dai painfully on the side of his face. Long hairs brushed his eyes. Slowly, slowly, movee foalee. Concentrate, you fool. Thought was anxiety, was concern, was almost fear.

He could feel the leg, inch by creeping inch, shifting under his hand. The foal was alive and moving too, and it twisted its body and the leg came forward easily, gently, slotting into position like the last piece of a jig-saw puzzle, just as the contractions speeded, and the mare stood, panting, wild-eyed, her body beyond all control, and the foal's head and forelegs slid smoothly from her into Dai's waiting hands. Two gentle pulls, and she had expelled the foal and was standing, shaking.

Kurt stood beside her, his hands stroking her, giving her time. Dai cut the foal's cord, after tying the tape, and applied antiseptic to the cut end, working as he always worked, quickly, deftly, with hands that obeyed him without question. His hands could work without his brain, and, now concentration was no longer needed, he was aware that the soreness in his throat was more than a hint that all was not well. It was a flaring pain that hurt when he breathed. His headache was worse and he wished the idiot bells would stop their incessant blaring. He wished he had not to face the long, dark drive home.

The foal was free from the membranes that covered its nose and mouth. Kurt was busy, experience guiding him. The presence of the two men was consolation to the mare. Soiled straw was carried away and fresh bedding tedded over the floor. Dai, examining her, was unhappy, and inserted a few stitches, as the foal had torn her during birth. She had been straining so long that she was exhausted. He stayed beside her until Kurt brought a warm bran and linseed mash. She fed gratefully, dipping her head. She had not yet looked at her foal.

The bells had stopped. Dai glanced at his watch. Midnight, and Christmas Day. He couldn't care less. Christmas was a nuisance, an interruption. Because of Christmas Kurt was single handed, and his employers were away, and Dai was thirty miles from home with a rising temperature, and an aching body and eyes that watered with tiredness. He longed for bed.

Kurt, glancing across at him, gave a small whistle of distress.

'You have flu, too,' he said.

'Probably,' Dai said. It hurt to talk. 'I'll manage. You'd better gargle. When's your headman due back?' His voice belonged to another man.

'Soon,' Kurt said. 'His wife say he get up today. I hope he

80

come back tomorrow. I have no sleep for two nights now. I cannot leave her. And the foal must feed soon. She has not looked at him.'

The foal was breathing easily. His ears moved as he looked around him. He was delicately made and handsome, a delightful reward for both of them. Dai dried the soft baby coat, as the mare made no move towards her offspring. She settled in the straw without a sign of interest.

The foal whickered.

The mare turned her head and stared at it, her ears flattened. She stood, trembling, and backed away. The foal's ears questioned the rustling straw. His amazed eyes looked at his new world. He tried to stand on rubbery legs, and fell again. The mare was terrified of him, and shied away, her eyes wild.

'We have trouble, oh yes!' Kurt said. His voice was flat and exhausted.

It was never easy to reconcile a reluctant animal to her young. The mare had had a bad time, had been badly frightened, and Kurt had already discovered that she was unusually temperamental, even for a racehorse. And the vet looked so ill.

The stableman went into the office, and poured coffee from a pan that was keeping warm on the electric hot-plate. Dai could not leave the mare until he was certain all was well. It was too long a drive to risk having to return, and Kurt could not manage alone. The flu epidemic could not have occurred at a more awkward time. Kurt added a tot of rum to each mug. Both of them could do with something to give them energy for the long hours that lay ahead. Dai drank slowly, red fire racing down his throat, so that his eyes watered even more. He began to feel sick. Kurt was whistling under his breath, trying to stifle worry.

'Stille Nacht, heilige Nacht,
Alles schläft, einsam wacht...'

Dai remembered the words from school. He was lightheaded. Words and the sound of bells floated through his mind.

Kurt rubbed the foal with salt. Perhaps the mare would lick the salt and all would be well. The little creature must feed.

'What's the mare's name?' Dai asked.

He had to keep his mind on the job, and forget his throat, and his aching body. Kurt also needed to talk. He was tired to death. Sleep was a dimly remembered luxury for which he would give all his wages.

'Lisa,' he said. 'I know another Lisa once, long ago in Austria, before the war. She, too, was very pretty.'

'Lisa,' Dai said.

He lifted the foal and held it in front of its mother. It could not yet stand alone. Its legs betrayed it as it struggled upwards, eyes gazing at the mare. It put its nose to hers. She started away again, trembling. She huffed at them, and the foal, amazed, made a small movement away from her. She backed against the wall, hating the creature that had invaded her stable, coming mysteriously from nowhere. She did not yet understand.

'He must feed soon,' Kurt said. The first feed was vital. 'I hold the mare and give her the rest of the mash. You hold the foal.'

It was only half successful, but luckily the foal knew his job and, once he found the full udder, sucked lustily. The mare stared at him, disliking the sensation, resenting his presence, but Kurt occupied her, feeding her, stroking her, praising her, telling her that all was well and she was beautiful and this was her foal, her little son, her treasure. The soft words interested her, and Dai received only two kicks on his shins before the foal stopped sucking and curled in the straw, nose to tail, forlorn and lonely. The mare moved to the far side of the foaling box, taking no interest at all in her son.

'We let them rest. Is warm in here. He do not hurt,' Kurt said, and Dai followed the little man into the office. The vet's face was burning, but he could not stop shivering. The rum and coffee had been a mistake; a wave of nausea caused him to close his eyes and drop heavily into a chair by the table, praying that the feeling would pass.

The shrilling telephone bell was an abomination.

Kurt answered, spoke briefly and rang off. Dai sat with his head in his hands. Death would be more merciful.

'Is William, our Head Man,' Kurt said. 'He has a flat across the yard. He wake and see the lights. He want me to go over. He has some tablets that help the flu. His wife bring them, and when she come, I go. He is worried. The mare is valuable. Is his responsibility. His wife do not let him come. Last year he have pleurisy.'

Dai nodded. It was too much effort to speak.

'Sit by the fire,' Kurt said anxiously. He helped Dai to the armchair, looking, on his way back to the desk, through the observation window. The mare had not moved.

A woman came in at the door, carrying a tray, on which was a plate of sandwiches, a thermos flask, a glass of water, and a small dish containing two large pills. She was small, grey-haired, and intensely vital. No one could ever ignore her.

'For goodness' sake go and see William and put him out of his misery, Kurt,' she said. 'It was all I could do to keep him from coming over here. Is the mare all right? You weren't hiding anything? He's been worrying about her all week, and he's annoyed too, as she's foaled much too early.'

Dai managed to nod. The foal would be a year old by racing standards on January 1st, although he was only a few days old in fact. And this meant that all his life he would be penalized by racing against his seniors. Unless he was very good, he would always be outclassed. It was bad luck that she had foaled so soon. Another few days and all would have been well.

The bells were ringing in his head again. The nausea returned. Damned bad luck. Flu was damned bad luck. Christmas was damned bad luck. He wished he was in bed. Everything was damned bad luck. He wished he was home, and how in hell was he going to drive thirty miles in the rain and the dark? The mare ... he ought to look at the mare. The foal wouldn't suck, the mare wouldn't suckle him, the foal ...

'Here,' the grey-haired woman said authoritatively, her voice penetrating the fog that was sweeping over Dai. 'These'll make you feel better. Don't worry. I'm a nurse, or was, and they're what the doctor gave my husband. They won't harm you at all.'

She watched Dai fumble with them, and held the glass for him to drink. It hurt merely to think of swallowing, let alone swallow.

'The mare,' Dai said thickly, as he handed back the glass.

She glanced through the observation window.

'She's lying quiet and the foal's asleep. I'm Mary Bennett,

but everyone calls me Mrs. William here. William's stable manager. Kurt was offered the job, as he's been here since the war, but he wouldn't take it. Said the men wouldn't like working under a foreigner, so William came two years ago.'

She poured coffee from the flask.

'Try and drink that. It will help.' She perched on the edge of the table. 'William adores horses. And horses detest me. Funny, isn't it? They've only got to see me, and they kick or bite. My own fault, I expect, as I've always been terrified of them. It's rough on William, as I can't help in an emergency. They react badly when I'm around.'

'How did you come to marry him?' Dai asked, forcing himself to listen. The nausea had receded, and was only a faint reminder, deep inside him.

'In wartime. I was a WAAF and he was in the RAF. I knew he worked with horses, but it didn't matter then. Life had no future. Remember?'

Dai remembered. Remembered being surprised during the blitz when he woke each morning to find himself alive; remembered night watches at sea, as he had been in the Marines for two years; remembered lying under fire on a beach in Italy, trying to kill a badly injured mule. He could not get into position to shoot the tormented animal. The remembered screams compounded with the bells, banging inside his head.

'Kurt's Austrian. He worked in a circus when he was a boy, looking after the Liberty horses. Then he went to work with the Lippizaner stallions at the Spanish Riding School in Vienna. Only he's Jewish. His wife and daughter vanished in the holocaust, and he landed in a concentration camp. He still has a number branded on his wrist.'

'Was his daughter called Lisa?' Dai asked, remembering what the little man had said.

Mrs. William nodded.

'Why?' she asked.

'The mare's name is Lisa. He said he knew a Lisa once. That she was pretty.'

Dai could not talk any more. He dozed, and startled into wakefulness when Kurt returned to the office. A small ginger kitten followed the groom to the fireplace, and climbed determinedly up Dai's trouser leg to roost blissfully on his knee, and purr loudly. The pills had already begun to work. The ache had receded, and his head felt clearer, though he was far from well.

'Mrs. William has gone to phone her brother. He is a news-agent in Trapperton. He drive you home. His son follow in their car, and bring his father back.'

'There's no need,' Dai said. 'It's too far for them.'

'There is need. You are ill. I have the flu first and know how ill. I give it to everyone else. Is a big nuisance. Everyone has flu here. The vet, even two of the doctors. Mrs. William also have it first, so she is better to nurse everyone else. And the mare's own groom, he is ill too. But Mrs. William has just ring him, and he say the mare like honey. Much honey. William say they expect trouble with this one. She is very flighty. Very naughty. But she learn.'

Dai rubbed his hand over his chin. He needed a shave. The kitten settled itself more comfortably. They would have to try again to get the mare to accept her foal. Kurt had brought a jar of honey back with him, and put some on a saucer, taking it into the foaling box. Dai put down the kitten and struggled to the doorway. His legs were made of paper and would buckle under him at any minute. He must ring Sheila and tell her to get hold of a locum. And that wouldn't be easy at Christmas. It was useless to pretend that he could carry on. It was years since he'd been ill. But this time he would have to give in. He had no option. The room was swinging round him. He stumbled across to watch the mare. She adored honey, having discovered it some months before, when her lad bought his wife a comb, and left it on a bench in her stable. She wolfed it all.

Kurt smeared the foal's head lavishly, before carrying the little creature to his mother, and laying him in the straw beside her. The foal flicked his ears, and she drew back, startled. The honey was close to her, was remembered delight, was a glorious mouth-watering smell in her nostrils. The foal's inquiring eyes turned towards her. She did not start away, but continued until there was no longer the slightest sweetness under her tongue.

The foal moved, seeking warmth. Kurt lifted him and put him against the mare's body. She turned her head. His smell reminded her of honey. She had caught his scent as she licked. he lifted his nose to hers, and she stared at him, her ears ques-tioning his presence, pointing towards him. Kurt stood, ready

85

to intervene. The foal whickered softly, and then sneezed. Recognition flared in the mare's eyes. She cuddled closer. A few minutes later, when Kurt glanced through the window, the foal was fast asleep, his mother's head stretched across his legs, her eyes half closed. There would be no more trouble.

Dai walked over to look through and reassure himself. He went wearily to lift the curtain and look out at the night. It was darker than death. He shivered, and stumbled to the armchair. The distant church clock struck five.

'Happy Christmas,' Kurt said ruefully. He sat down at the desk. 'Mrs. William's brother come at six. It will be a busy Christmas for some. A miserable Christmas for others. Yet we make fun and make merry. Is odd.'

He sat, a weary little man, a lonely man, exiled, among strangers, remembering.

'Christmas is for children. When my Lisa is small, she love the tree. We have one big one, in the living-room. When the Christmas bells sounded, the tree lights go on.' He looked at the past, brooding.

'At Christmas I am always glad to work,' he went on. 'The horses, they know none of this. They cannot say things that hurt. And little foals do not remind me of little children.

Dai did not answer. There was nothing that could be said. He was mesmerized by the imitation flames, and wondered uneasily how man could speak of goodwill once a year, and, year after year, could turn his words into such mockery that, a few days after the festival, the sentiments were forgotten, all as spurious as the continual electric flicker in the hearth in front of him.

86

CHAPTER TWELVE

DAI remembered little of the long drive home, except that it seemed endless. He drifted in and out of uneasy sleep, waking to see the long headlights cutting the dark. His driver, Mrs. William's brother, was a taciturn man at the best of times and, having never driven a Land-Rover before, had to concentrate on his task, and did not speak one word on the drive. Behind them, his son followed in the family estate wagon. They both wanted to be home again as soon as possible, as the son's children would expect their Christmas presents.

Dai insisted on driving up to his own house from the gate, not wanting to delay them. If they came to the house, Sheila would invite them in, and it would not be easy to refuse. He felt that he had taken enough of their time. He waved to his escort as they drove away, wishing he knew how to thank them properly. As it was, he was glad to see them go. He climbed into his vehicle and drove into the yard just as Sheila let the cats out into the morning murk.

Elliott, dazzled by the headlights, became bewildered, and ran towards Dai, who saw the cat, cursed, and twisted the wheel too hard. Two seconds later the Land-Rover hit a tree. Elliott, terrified by the crash, streaked for the house, and ran inside as Sheila opened the door again and raced down the drive. Dai stared at her blearily. Blood trickled down his face from the cut on his head, but he was otherwise unhurt. He stumbled into the kitchen, where Susie stared at him in horror. She had never known her father ill before.

Dai never remembered how he got to bed. He woke once to see the doctor standing beside him, and managed to croak an apology for picking such a lousy time to have flu. He was vaguely aware, some hours later, of an unfamiliar voice outside his bedroom door, and even more vaguely aware that Sheila said they had been lucky and got a locum straight away. He slept, and roused briefly, to drink gallons of home-made lemon-ade, and to sleep again. It was not until the fourth day after the visit to the stables that he woke clear-headed, and began to worry about his practice.

He hammered on the floor. No one was bothering about him. He wanted a wash. He wanted a shave. He wanted a drink and nobody cared. Nobody had looked into the room for hours. Intense misery overwhelmed him. Someone might have come to see if he was awake.

Tim raced upstairs.

'Mum's got flu, Dad,' he said. 'She's in bed in my room, and I'm sleeping with Mark. Susie's been ill as well. I think I had it first, only it wasn't bad. I suppose I gave it to you all. The doctor's coming soon. And Mum got you a locum. His name's Michael Langford. Did you want something?'

'What about the animals?' Dai asked. 'And how's the mare over at Trapperton, and for heaven's sake who's running this place?'

Tim sat down on the edge of the bed.

'It's all right. Michael's a jolly good bloke. He went over to see the mare the day after you got ill, and now her own vet's back. And they've got equine flu at the riding stables. Mollie hasn't been home for four days. Do you want some food? It's a bit of a hit and miss affair without Mum or Mollie, but I can do toast.'

'That must be difficult,' Dai commented acidly. There was an automatic toaster in the kitchen.

Tim laughed.

'Don't worry. Bess Logan came up to help out. She's always ratty, but she doesn't really mean it, and she's a jolly good cook. She made some bone broth for you when you began to feel like food. She says there's nothing like bone broth. I'll bring you some up. She won't go into men's bedrooms. And would you like to see Michael when surgery finishes? He says he's been inoculated against flu, so he won't get it.'

'I hope he's right,' Dai said, wishing his son felt less talk-ative. Tim was only garrulous when everyone else wanted silence.

It was frustrating to lie upstairs, listening to sounds in the house, and trying to identify them. A strange dog barked, and there was a Siamese cat in the surgery. He could hear its yowls. Its voice was quite unlike Tia's or Elliott's. Tim had left the bedroom door ajar. A few minutes later a sleek paw slipped through, and a head followed, pushing the door open. Elliott gazed at Dai, walked over to the bed, and jumped on to the eiderdown, curling himself contentedly. The vet remembered the small black shape caught in the headlights, and put his hand to his face. It hurt to touch, and was bandaged. He wrinkled his forehead, and knew that the cut had been stitched. He grinned wryly. What a way to spend Christmas. When was Christmas? He must have missed it all.

Michael Langford shut the surgery door after the last animal had departed and walked into the kitchen. Bess was preparing a tray on which was thin toast, made under the grill as she didn't trust them pop-ups, they always made her jump, and they did the toast too hard. She put the broth in a mug, thinking it easier to drink that way, when a man was in bed, and added Michael's cup of coffee to the tray.

'He's awake, and he's worrying,' Bess said tersely. 'Young Mollie phoned from the stables. There's another horse coughing badly and she's not sure the one you saw yesterday isn't starting pneumonia.'

'I'll be right over,' Michael said.

He took the tray and went upstairs. Dai had managed to push his pillows into a more comfortable position and was sitting up. He felt well enough to be irritated by the bristles on his chin, and conscious of being unwashed as well as unshaven. His throat was better, but his legs still ached. He looked up at his locum as the door opened and Michael Langford smiled, a little uncertainly. It had been far from easy, taking over without any briefing, and at such short notice, and he had only qualified the summer before. He had taken a job abroad for a few months, to gain experience, and come home to have a quiet Christmas and then try and find an assistantship. He grinned. Some quiet Christmas. He put the tray down carefully on Dai's knees. Dai, looking up, saw a tall fair man, wearing horn-rimmed spectacles. He seemed little older than Tim.

'Bess says you're to drink every drop,' Michael said.

'It looks disgusting,' Dai commented, glancing at the thin yellow brew in the mug.

'It's not, actually. I had some last night. It'll do you good.'
Michael lapsed into his surgery manner, and Dai laughed.

'I'm not a dog. How's the practice? And what about that
mare and her foal over at Trapperton?'

'Both fine. Mr. Hamilton's better now. He rang to thank you
and said you did a great job.' Dai had a moment's puzzlement
before he identified Dougal. He nodded.

'And what about flu at the stables?'

'That's pretty bad,' Michael said. 'And half the staff are off
with human flu. Luckily they only seem to be getting it mildly
and they've all been back in two days. I think Mollie had it, but
if she did she managed to keep it pretty dark. The flu started on
Boxing Day. They've had nine horses taken ill in the last four
days. They're all pretty tired, and there's so much night nursing
and they don't have enough staff. The girls look whacked. The
stable owner is working right round the clock, but now his
wife's ill. She carried on too long. It's a vicious bug if you do
that. Trouble is they can't really isolate the horses, as the loose
boxes are all next to each other. It's running through the lot like
wildfire, and there's a possible case of pneumonia.'

'You'd best get over there.'

Dai was already tired by talking, and he cursed himself. He
wasn't going to be back this week, and maybe not next. He
should have packed in sooner, but how the hell could he?

'I'll come up and see you this evening if surgery's not too
busy,' Michael said. 'You needn't worry. I can cope with most
of it. All your beasts seem well. Deedee's been lying outside
your door, fretting. Mark's just taken her for a walk, but maybe
she can come in and see you when they get back. The little fox
is O.K. He's never left Susie day or night except for a short run
in the garden.'

'Has Mark had flu?' Dai asked.

'He spent a couple of days feeling seedy.' Michael walked to
the window and looked out over the fells. He was used to softer
country, to the Sussex downland and friendly woods. The bleak
moors appalled him.

'Half the village is down with it.' He did not add that Steve
Johns had been very ill, and was now in hospital with pneumonia. Michael had been over to Deep Willows two days
before to treat a sickly calf. Sheila had told him about Deep

Willows before she had been forced to give up and go to bed. She had hung on as long as she could. Michael had been concerned when he visited, as Lysbeth was worked off her feet, and Stan Turner was ill.

Life was difficult for everyone. Although he had only been there four days Michael had already learned to watch the sky anxiously, worrying about snow. The stables could easily be cut off, and he needed to keep a close eye on all the horses. Driving across the fells, he wondered how Dai ever coped. It was far too big a practice for one man. Perhaps Mr. Evans would let him stay on.

Tim had said they were looking for an assistant. The advertisement was due in the veterinary journal this week. It was the sort of practice Michael wanted. His father had been a country vet, with a farming practice, and he had grown up in a house like the House of Beasts, and had often helped with emergencies. His mother died when he was nine, and his father had taken him with him whenever he could, concerned that his son should not grow up too lonely.

Michael had had plenty of experience before he started college, and knew exactly what his life would be once he was qualified. He had no romantic notions of a glorious profession. He knew that he would spend his time in down to earth and often unspeakable conditions, doing unspeakable things in appalling surroundings, frozen in winter, baked and surrounded by flies and stinks in summer. It was all he wanted. He had no illusions whatever.

He had hoped to inherit his father's practice, but his father died of a coronary brought on by overwork when Michael was in his second year at college; there was a new man in his old home now. He offered Michael a job but there were too many memories, and he could not bear the house now that his father was dead. There was enough work at the House of Beasts for three men, let alone two. If only Dai Evans liked him. If only they could get on.

Michael had little confidence, and there was another reason too, but he was not yet admitting it, even to himself. His visit to the stables was more than a routine. He looked forward, with unaccustomed excitement, to seeing Mollie Evans again. There was something very appealing about the small slight girl with her delicately tanned skin, wide candid eyes, and dark ponytail. And she was a wizard with horses.

He jumped out of the Land-Rover as he reached Deep Willows, which was on the way to the riding stables. As he strode across the yard, head up, eyes gleaming, the embodiment of vigour, Lysbeth, walking wearily out of the dairy, where she had been writing up the cattle records, looked at him and thought suddenly, 'Lord, lord, what it is to be young.'

CHAPTER THIRTEEN

It was ten days before Dai was well again. Michael went out to do the house visits, and Dai started his old routine, pleased to be working, though he was unduly tired when he finished surgery. He dropped into the big armchair in the kitchen, and Deedee came straight to him, and rested her head on his knee. She hated people staying in bed. She never liked change in the house routine, and had been badly upset because both Dai and Sheila were ill. Nothing like that had ever happened before in her life.

Bess stayed on, pleased to be of use. Sheila, shaky still, but better, was sitting at the kitchen table, engrossed in her library books. She had phoned Lysbeth earlier that day. Steve seemed to be improving, but he still had no interest in anything. He did not want to hear about the farm, or to talk about coming home, and the doctor had suggested leaving him in hospital for another week. It was not good hearing. Ted Wellans sent out one of his own men to help Lysbeth with the cattle, and Ted and Rob Hinney were both working overtime at Sheerlings as a result. Ted visited Lysbeth daily to see if she had any problems that he could solve, and she was grateful, but their major worry was still the proposed scheme to build a reservoir in the valley. The hearing had been postponed because half the officials concerned were ill with flu.

The telephone rang and Dai went to answer it.

'Mr. Evans?'

It was Michael's voice.

'I'm out at the little farm at the end of Hortonmere — Throcken End. They have four sick calves, and I haven't seen this illness before. Are you well enough to come over if Mrs. Evans doesn't need her car? I'd like you to see them. If you come over I can get along to the stables. I was on

93

my way there, but Throcken End rang me while I was at Wellans, and I came straight over.'

Dai rang off thoughtfully. The flu epidemic at the stables had almost run its course, but two horses had nasty coughs and one, with pneumonia, was only making a slow recovery. Mollie had come home for three days, most of which she spent asleep, and went back again. There was so much nursing to do. All the horses were rugged and none could go outside. A bitter wind, straight from the depths of hell, screamed over the fells. There were medicines to give, and inhalations to prepare, and the straw to muck out, and the work was endless. Mucking out alone took hours when the horses were inside, as the floors of the loose boxes had to be cleaned around them. Mollie's hands were raw, and she was outside in all weathers, as she was head groom, overseeing everybody. She mixed the feed and kept the records, and Dai knew that his daughter, like himself, never spared time or energy till all the animals were tended. Looking at her, during her stay at home, he had wondered whether she had bothered to eat in the last few days. Irritation seethed in him, as he felt that she was imposed on by the stable owners, who did not, in their turn, make sure the girls were properly fed and rested. He dismissed Mollie from his mind. He must get to Throcken End.

Sheila answered absently when he spoke, and he went out to her car feeling hard-done-by. Every irritating little detail was magnified out of all proportion, and he hoped none of his surgery patients would come to him neglected, because he was in no state to guard his tongue. One day it would get him into trouble.

The road at the end of Hortonmere was little more than a track. The farm at Throcken End was small, a stone house, simple as a child's drawing, two windows and a door between, squatting under menacing peaks that were its sole horizon. The mountains brooded above it, close and dark. Dai always hated the place. He climbed out of the station wagon to battle with a leaning gate that sagged wearily from one hinge. It opened, reluctantly, creaking horribly. A thin collie ran at him, barking, and quietened again as it caught his scent and recognized him.

Dai looked about him. Nothing was well done or properly

repaired, not through neglect, but exhaustion. Not enough time. Not enough care. Not enough money. Not only the beasts suffered, but also Jack Grey and his wife and family. Ella Grey met him by the duck pond, where three muddy white ducks quacked noisily, and a small mallard rooted in the mud. Dai bent to look at the mallard, which was a drake, and the bird left the pond and waddled towards him.

'He's got to know us all,' Ella said. 'He was shot, and landed in the field over there. He's better now, but he won't go. I reckon we'll have half-wild birds next year. I don't know if they do inter-breed.'

She was leading the way to the calf pens, talking nervously, a thin little woman with tired eyes, and hands that were redder than Mollie's, and raw with sores. It was a wicked life, out there in the wilds, miles from anywhere. Dai wondered if she ever saw another woman, or enjoyed a chat with a friend, or brought herself a pretty trifle. Certainly Jack would never think to buy her one, any more than he himself ever remembered to buy something for Sheila, though one day he'd surprise her. He sighed. Life was a race against time and circumstance and the weeks sped so fast that it was Monday again before a man realized the last week was ended.

The yard at Throcken End had never been paved, and winter had not improved it. It was thick with mud, and deep in cow-dung. No hosing could ever clean it. Dai glanced at the store bullocks. They were fat enough and there was plenty of winter feed in the barn. The cows were in a paddock, long denuded of grass. They milled wearily, deep in mud that plastered their legs.

'We're building a winter shed,' Ella explained.

It hurt her to see the beasts so poorly kept, but what could she do? It had taken long enough to persuade the bank to give them a loan to put the new buildings up, and now there was a strike at the contractors', and heaven knew when the roof would be finished. Nothing ever went smoothly.

She led the way, conscious of her appearance, trying to hide her hands under her apron. Dai felt pity stir him, and followed her, wishing he could shed his feelings. Life was so damned unfair. The Greys worked until they were dropping with tired-ness, and did no harm to anyone. They'd be better selling up.

But Jack was not trained for any other life. At best he could hope for a job as cowman on another farm. The jungle law still operated in modern life and only the fittest survived. But who were the fittest? Dai pushed his thoughts away. The flu had left him maudlin.

The calves were in loose boxes, in a building by themselves. Dai went in to look at them, noticing that here Ella and Jack had done their utmost to ensure that everything was as clean as possible, the walls whitewashed, the straw newly spread, and each calf isolated. Dai looked at them with an expert eye.

'How long have they been sick?' he asked.

'The first one went off its feed three days ago. We bought this lot from the Sales. My brother used to sell us his calves, but he's had to pack up. He couldn't make ends meet, nohow. Looks like we might follow, if things don't get better,' Ella said.

Dai opened the first calf's mouth. He was almost sure of what he would see, and was not surprised to find the little beast had a swollen tongue and grey fungoid-like patches at the back of its throat.

'It's calf diphtheria,' he said.

'Diphtheria?' Ella stared at him. 'Will they die? And what about our own calves? I've kept them separate, but . . .'

'I don't know. We'll try penicillin, and you'll have to nurse them carefully. Keep them isolated, whatever you do, and either get Jack to see to the other calves and keep away from these, or scrub up thoroughly and change your clothes before you go near the rest of them.'

'Jack's seeing to them,' Ella said. 'I'll do my best. Don't worry about that, Mr. Evans.'

Dai nodded. Ella always did. It was circumstances, not people, causing trouble here. She and Jack both worked every hour of every day, and part of the night too, if necessary, but the land was starvation poor, under the mountain, where rock bones showed through the ground, and ploughing was a penance, and winter an Arctic nightmare that could scarcely be endured.

The farmhouse kitchen, though small, was warm and friendly. A fire blazed, a cat stretched on the rug, and the dog, accompanied by a small child, had come indoors. Both were watching Dai suspiciously. He warmed his hands, but refused a cup of coffee, knowing Ella had little spare time. The diphtheria was a disaster, and it meant visiting daily for the next week or so, and what was more, it meant free visiting, as there was never enough money at Throcken End to meet all the bills. Jack paid when he could, a little on account here, a little on account there. Ella walked to the gate with Dai, stopping at the dairy to pick a dozen eggs out of a basket. She gave them to the vet. It was something on account.

'Don't worry,' Dai said, but that was useless advice. The calves meant money wasted. If Ella was lucky they would recover, but the chances were evens against them thriving. Depression settled down on him again as he drove home. His thoughts were as bleak as the grey sodden fells that had never seemed so forbidding, where the mountains behind them were crouched beasts of prey, waiting to spring. The sky pressed down on him, promising more snow. All they needed now was a snow storm to make life unendurable, and the thought had barely crossed his mind when the first flakes flickered against the windscreen, and the world was narrowed to a few yards of moorland on either side.

CHAPTER FOURTEEN

THIS time, the snow lay deep for days. There was no respite. Snow was disaster. Snow was buried sheep and isolated houses, and farms that were unreachable. Snow was Ella Grey, running out of medicines, nursing four sick calves. Snow was the stables, where a horse had pneumonia, and Mollie was marooned, and Michael and Dai were unable to reach her. Snow was Ned getting up each morning, to go out with Sable to find buried sheep. Snow was misery, was sick men without a doctor, was the farmer's wife at Seven Elms starting labour while the ambulance men fought to reach her, and her husband delivered the child single-handed. Luckily mother and son were healthy and came to no harm.

Snow was abandoned lorries and cars on the fell road; snow was drivers trudging miserably into Dai's kitchen, blue with cold, blowing on frozen fingers, being fed, and warmed with scalding tea, and sent to the Swan where snow, for Mrs. Jones, was work unending, as the Huntsman was helping dig out the sheep, and she was alone.

Snow was children unable to go to school, and no lights on the more remote farms as the electricity cables were down. Machinery had to be operated, if it could, by emergency generators, or by tractor engines. Snow was the helicopter overhead, dropping provisions to the farms, and feed to the ponies wintering wild on the fells. The deer, too, came to share the ponies' hay. Snow was cold feet and cold hands and cold homes when the coke lorries failed to deliver.

Snow was one of Bess's cats dying in a snowdrift. Snow was constant fear of being lost, of thaw, of flooding. Snow was a hidden valley, where each man nursed his own private worries. Dai and Michael worked where they could. They tried, and failed, to get through to Throcken End, which was not on the telephone. Jack Grey had to drive two miles to a neighbour to ring the vet, but now he was completely isolated. They tried, and failed, to get through to Mollie at the stables. They tried, and failed, to reach Lysbeth at Deep Willows.

Snow was a pensioner dying of cold in her damp cottage in Back Lane. Dai, passing on foot, as vehicles were useless, heard a dog howling, and looked in at the window. A moment later, he broke the pane, lifted the latch, and jumped through. The old woman was lying on the floor. He was too late. She had been dead for hours. The whimpering pup walked towards him, shivering. There was an empty bowl by the ash-filled hearth, and several pools on the floor, showing that the animal had been there alone for some time. Dai could do nothing. He tucked the pup inside his coat, and walked to the police house. He went home after making his statement, and was angrier than he could remember. Somebody should have known; somebody should have called; somebody should have seen she had fuel and food. He had looked in the pantry, where there was nothing, only a loaf of bread, a half-empty packet of tea, and three tins of dogfood.

He reached home, and snapped at Sheila when she asked him if he was ready for his lunch. Michael was eating, his face a grey mask of tiredness. He had never worked so hard in his life, and was walking everywhere, trying to get to the farms, trying to do whatever he could. He had shovelled snow for three pensioners trapped in their cottages, and shopped for another two, as well as doing his own job.

Dai put the pup on the mat. Elliott stared at it, and sniffed it, and the pup backed towards Dai, knowing his smell. Everything here was strange. Deedee walked regally towards it, and put a firm paw on it. It stared up at her, and rolled on its back, suppliant. Deedee lay down with a deep sigh of content. At last she had a pup of her own. She licked its face, and it relaxed. Dai brought food, which it ate greedily, asking for more, but he did not want to overload it. He had no idea how long it had been unfed. It was a pretty little creature, obviously well cared for and well loved. Susie, coming into the room, her cheeks bright from tobogganing, knelt beside the pup with a sigh of pure bliss.

'Is it ours?' she asked.

She turned, and saw Dai's face. His expression was bleak. He could still feel the tiny body of the old woman in his hands. She had weighed no more than a sparrow, just skin and bone, dying alone and untended. Susie crept to her father's side and rubbed her cheek against his face. She was cold, and he had not seen her approach and he was startled.

'I do love you,' Susie said.

Michael choked over his meat. He fitted into the family so well that he was almost one of them, arguing with Tim over the merits of various football teams, helping Mark with his homework, fetching Mollie from the stables, and playing with Susie, who adored him. He had never been so happy in his life as in the past weeks. If only he could stay. He watched Susie, who had long ago discovered how to wheedle her father into giving her a good deal of her own way.

'Cupboard love,' Dai said, knowing perfectly well what was happening, but, for once, enjoying it. It took away the sour taste of the morning.

'Whose pup is it?' Michael asked.

Dai lifted his hand quickly turning the thumb down, out of Susie's sight. Michael hastily changed the subject, guessing at tragedy, which happened only too often. Susie sat beside Deedee, stroking the pup's soft fur. It licked her hand.

'We'll call him . . .' Susie paused. 'What kind is he?'

'Beagle, I should think,' Dai said. 'And he's a her.'

'Candy,' Susie said. 'Candy . . . you must learn your name.' The pup wagged its tail, delighted to be noticed. The last two days had been very lonely, as well as cold and frightening.

'It should probably be called Snowfall,' Sheila said.

She began to clear away, and Susie fetched a book to read to the dogs. She loved reading aloud, and was always hurt when told to be quiet, as her voice was far from soothing. Now, no one checked her, and Deedee seemed to listen, and the pup slept, warm, and safe, and comfortable.

Dai followed Sheila into the scullery, and Michael, clearing the table, came out in time to hear how Dai had found the pup. Sheila stared up at him, sudden tears in her eyes.

'Oh, Dai,' was all she could say, and the vision haunted her, of the old lady there alone, ill, unvisited, trying to the last to ensure that the pup was fed. She felt so miserable that she walked to the Vicarage to talk to the vicar's wife, and by nightfall there was a rota of villagers willing to visit other old people. Everyone was shocked by the story.

'It's just that nobody thinks till something like this happens,' Mrs. Jones said that night, in the Swan, where each man sat wondering if he too were culpable. There were many long uneasy silences.

Frost had clamped over the snow, and it had been colder than indifference for the last three nights. Men went home early, to sit by blazing fires, and shiver, unable to forget the picture that Dai had painted in words that shrivelled them all, so that they shared his feeling of guilt.

The vet stayed behind for a word with Mrs. Jones. Michael, leaving a few minutes ahead of him, returned with a burly dark-haired man wearing a thick duffle coat.

'I 'ad to leave the lorry,' the dark man said. 'I need a bed for the night. Road's blocked.' He looked hopefully at Mrs. Jones, but she had a house full of stranded travellers.

'Better come with us,' Dai said. 'If you don't mind having a blanket, and sleeping on the kitchen chair, with the animals.'

'I breed greyhounds,' the lorry driver said, as he followed them into the street. 'So long as I'm warm I don't care where I sleep, even if it's in the kennel with the dog.'

Moonlight silvered the snow. Moonlight shimmered on frosted trees, on encrusted branches glittering against windows etched by icy flowers. Moonlight shone from a clear sky in which stars were chilly sparks flashing from blind distances that were infinitely frightening. A chill wind whipped at Dai's face, and wild instincts, bequeathed by far-off ancestors, gripped him, paralysing thought. For one terrifying minute he was alone in an alien world and there was nothing, anywhere, but bleak fells, the unending snow, and the vast empty night, and he was a minute and unconsidered speck, without identity.

His companion's words restored him abruptly to the present.

'I'm Joe Harker,' the lorry driver said, as they turned in at the gateway of the House of Beasts, and floundered along the slippery path. 'I drive a lorry for a haulage firm. Not much fun in this weather.'

The house lights welcomed them. Sheila had prepared a casserole for supper, and she fetched an extra plate. Deedee and

Candy came to greet the stranger, smiling at him, smelling the scent of his own dogs, strong on his clothing. He fussed over them, revelling in warmth and company after long hours spent driving through snow, alone in his cab. He too had sensed the terror of emptiness earlier that evening.

Sheila checked the animals in the barn, and ensured that all was well with them, and that they were safe for the night. Conker greeted her with a delighted whinny, asking for the half carrot that was always given him at bedtime. Sheila patted him. He was growing old, and was not eating well. She was glad that he ate his carrot. It had become his special treat over the years.

Susie had been in bed for some time. Mollie was still marooned at the stables. Tim, who was studying for his 'O' levels that year, had retreated to the study to work. Mark, who had been struggling with his project on the Romans in the Lake District, was sitting wishing he had not eaten any supper.

'I feel sick,' he said.

'You eat too much.' His mother was unsympathetic.

'Like my lad.' The lorry driver laughed. 'I always tell Terry he's got hollow legs. Don't know where he puts it all. You go up to bed and lie flat on your back, son, and you'll be right as ninepence in no time.'

Mark went off miserably, followed by Sheila. Dai fetched blankets and a pillow for the visitor while the cats and dogs watched with interest. Elliott and Candy thought a new game had been invented for their delectation and crept under the blanket, to spring at one another, Elliott patting, and Candy biting playfully, till they ended with a romp and a roll. Rusty joined in, growling. Joe was intrigued by the fox and snapped his fingers at him. Rusty came to lean against the lorry driver's leg. He liked people who liked him.

'Leave them be,' Joe said. 'They make good company.' He flicked a finger, and Candy, delighted, growled and pretended to bite.

It was later than Dai had realized. He watched Elliott settle on Joe's lap, and Tia and Sim curl up together. He walked to the window and lifted the curtain. It was snowing again, large flakes falling from a sky that was almost clear. It could not last. Snow slithered from the roof, startling them all. Deedee barked.

'There's plenty of wood,' Dai said. 'Keep the fire in, or you'll be cold. I'm afraid we haven't any more blankets.'

'I've slept in my cabin before now with no heat at all,' Joe said. 'Don't worry. I'll be O.K.'

He dwarfed the chair, a big, capable, tough-looking man. Dai nodded good night and went upstairs. The house settled itself to sleep.

Dai woke an hour later, and sat up, startled. Someone was sobbing. He switched on the light and ran to the door, seeing Mark's bedroom light shining under the crack and across the landing. He hurried into the room and stared down at his son. Mark was doubled up, knees against his chin, hands gripped between his knees. His face was an old man's face, grey-green, tight over the bones, wide, frightened eyes staring, as sobs racked him.

'Hey, hey,' Dai said. 'A pain?'

Mark nodded.

Sheila, coming hastily into the room, shrugging on her housecoat, took one look at her son, and turned and stared at Dai.

'Stay with him,' Dai said. 'I'll ring the doctor.'

Sheila followed her husband on to the landing.

'Appendicitis,' she said softly. 'Oh, Dai.'

'He'll be all right. But don't leave him.' Dai's voice was rough, and he pushed her into the room and shut the door. He took the stairs two at a time, forgetting Joe, who started up in alarm as the light flooded the room.

'Kid's got appendicitis,' Dai said. He didn't want to think further. It looked more like peritonitis, and miles of snow lay between them and the hospital. He didn't know if the doctor could get through.

Joe flung off his blanket and put the cats on the rug. All of them had come to share his warmth.

'What can I do?' he asked, and Dai tried to think rationally.

'Kettle. Make us some tea, please.'

He was already at the phone, praying the lines weren't down, praying for someone to answer. God, what a time for disaster. He should have noticed that Mark was always feeling sick these days. And they'd thought it was greed. Hell and damnation.

The ringing bell was never ending, sounding in a sleeping house. Time was a narrow thread, spinning to infinity. The House of Beasts was a trap, filled with terror. A clock struck two. A voice answered. At last.

'I think Mark's got peritonitis,' Dai said.

There was a silence, followed by a startled oath.

'I'll be right over,' John Linney said. He knew everyone in the village. He'd delivered most of the children and closed the eyes of their grandparents.

'Can you get through?' Dai asked.

'I'll get through.'

There was nothing to do but wait. Joe filled two cups with hot tea and Dai took them upstairs. Sheila held both Mark's hands in hers, trying to stifle panic. They were so helpless. She felt as if she had been sitting for hours, watching Mark suffer, and she could do nothing. She murmured to him, soothing him as best she could, fighting tears, which would alarm the boy. The clock struck the quarter. She had only been with him for fifteen minutes. If only they'd realized how often he did feel sick, but he had never complained of pain.

'Dad?' It was a croak from an infinite distance. Dai wrapped a hot water bottle in a towel and put it in the bed, placing it carefully to warm his son's icy feet, and gripped Mark's shoulder hard.

'You'll be O.K. soon, son,' he said, and managed a friendly grin, though his lips felt stiff and he himself had an ache in his throat and blind terror in his heart. Michael put an anxious head round the door. He had heard noises and gone downstairs to investigate. Joe, unable to sleep again, was brewing tea, for want of a better occupation. He told Michael about Mark.

'Hey, old man,' Michael said, as he bent over and ruffled the boy's hair. 'You'll be over this in no time.'

He went out again, and Dai followed him downstairs. Joe poured more tea and handed it to them, but Dai could not drink. He paced the kitchen, counting the dawdling minutes, worrying the animals, who followed him with their eyes.

Michael said nothing. He had been shocked when he saw Mark, who looked as if death had already claimed him. He sat and stared at the fire, while Joe waited with them, and watched helplessly.

The ringing doorbell startled them all. Dai answered it, while Michael quieted the dogs, and then faced Joe across the kitchen table, listening to the hurrying footsteps on the stairs. Tim came down, hair on end, brown eyes worried.

'What's going on?'

'Your father thinks Mark's got appendicitis,' Michael said.

'Oh, glory. Poor old Mark. How will they get him to hospital?'

It was a question that Michael had been asking himself. He stared out of the window at the endless vista of dark, where snow-covered roads and lanes, mountains and fells, fields and hollows, cut them off completely. They were isolated, helpless as any village in the Middle Ages. Civilization was only a memory.

Dr. Linney came into the kitchen and nodded to them. Joe, feeling he must help somehow, knowing how he would feel if his own son were lying upstairs, poured another cup of tea and passed it to the doctor, who was already at the telephone dialling. Michael took a second cup of tea up to Sheila, and met Dai on the stairs.

'We've only one hope,' Dai said. 'The helicopter.'

Back in the kitchen, moments lengthened to hours. The animals slept. Michael tried to read, but the words danced in front of his eyes. Dai sat, and stood, and sat again, and went to the window and stared towards the village, but saw nothing. John Linney returned upstairs and sat opposite Sheila, his eyes on Mark. He had given the boy some tablets to ease the pain. Now there was nothing to do but wait. Sheila, holding Mark's hands, smiled at him when he turned his head and managed a shaky smile.

'You'll soon be in the helicopter,' Sheila said. 'That'll be fun, won't it?'

Mark nodded. He was in a world of his own, where pain was paramount and nothing made sense. Sim had come upstairs and jumped on the bed. Mark stroked the cat's smooth fur, deriving a little comfort as Sim purred.

A few minutes later the village policeman knocked on the door.

'I've got hold of the District Nurse,' he said. 'She'll go with him. They want us to get him to the Church Green. I've got a gang clearing the snow, and they can land there. We've got the Green ringed with cars, and all their headlights are on. Everything's ready.'

Dai wrapped Mark in blankets. Joe, in the kitchen, brought his blanket too and put it round the child.

'Let me carry him,' he said. 'I'm used to heavier weights than this, and he's only a flyweight, aren't you, son?'

The helicopter engine sounded overhead. It was time to leave.

Sheila watched the small procession disappear into the darkness. Dai and Michael were leading, their big torches lighting the path. She sat down in the armchair, shivering with the fear that she had so far kept at bay. Deedee put her head on her mistress's knee, sensing her misery. Elliott jumped up, purring, and Sheila lifted the little cat and held him tight, remembering the night that he had climbed on to the roof, and Mark had rescued him.

'Oh, Mark, Mark,' she whispered.

A moment later the cat scrambled free, startled. He had not realized before that it could rain indoors.

CHAPTER FIFTEEN

No one slept. Morning came, but not relief from fear. Dai, standing in the surgery, wished that the waiting-room was full, wished there was work to fill the endless hours before there could be any news. The helicopter had taken Mark to Bradford. Dai looked out at the snow, at the fells, rolling for miles, bleak, forbidding. If the valley were flooded, he would not care. He would leave and find a practice where winter was not a penance, where there were men and lorries to clear the snow, where children were not at risk. He could not settle to anything.

Tim fed the animals and cleaned the kennels, and stood with his arms round Conker, savouring his warmth, and the pleasant smell of horse, needing comfort, but too old to ask for it from his parents. Too old for tears, but never too old for terror. Old Mark. Nutty old Mark, who'd spent a night lost on his own house roof; maddening Mark, who interrupted and shouted and borrowed Tim's books and tools without permission and never remembered where he'd left them; Mark, who flared into sudden rages and lashed out in fury over nothing, who half killed a boy for kicking a dog in the village street. It wasn't fair. It wasn't fair. It was a beastly world, and nothing was fair.

Michael, putting his head in at the door, saw Tim standing motionless, one arm round Conker's neck, and withdrew hastily. He himself felt sick. Dai and Sheila had made him welcome, had made him feel part of their family, and Mark and Tim and Susie were fun, making up for a part of life that he, as an only child, had missed. The friendly quarrels, the noise, the laughter, had been wonderful. Now they were stilled, and Sheila was walking the house like a zombie, barely noticing anyone, and Susie sat silent, frightened by her parents' total abstraction. No one dared tell her the truth. No one wanted to face the possibilities. Neither Dai nor Sheila could think of anything but Mark, flying off into the night, lying ill among strangers. Sheila wished she could have gone with him, but there was no room in the helicopter. Besides, heaven knows when the snow would clear and let her come back, and she could not leave Susie.

Joe, unable to shift his lorry, stayed on, sleeping in Mark's bed. He helped wherever he could, playing endless games of draughts with Susie, talking to her, and listening to her while she read aloud. He had a small daughter of his own, and was clever with young children. Tim wished his sister were older. It was bad enough to know that Mark was so ill that he had to be rushed off in the middle of the night to hospital, in a helicopter, without having to keep his fears to himself. If Susie started one of her tantrums, because she thought Mark might die . . .

Tim left Conker and went into the garden. He spent an hour making snowballs, hurling them with all his might against the trunk of a tree. Susie wanted to go out and play too, but Joe, watching Tim, knew the play was too rough, and that Tim was taking out his misery in action. Snow splattered all over the garden.

The postman, coming up the drive, carrying his whippet bitch, was a welcome distraction, and Michael and Dai almost collided as they went to meet him. The bitch was expecting pups. She was slender, and too finely built for nature to have her way.

'Caesarian,' Dai said.

Michael would have liked to operate, but Dai needed occupation. Michael stood watching, admiring the deft hands that worked so swiftly. The tiny stitches were almost invisible when the operation was complete, and five pups lay in a box, with a padded hot water bottle beneath them, and an infra-red lamp above, the blind heads moving towards the warmth, minute paws grabbing at one another as they gained strength.

It passed an hour for both of them, and gave them satisfaction, but the hour had been endless for Sheila. If only she had thought about Mark's frequent sickness. If only she had taken him to the doctor. There had never been time. It was all her fault. Bess Logan, coming up when she heard the news, took one look at Sheila, and scolded her sharply.

'No use wishing past were different,' she said. 'And any fool can be wise to hindsight. We'll spring-clean the waiting-room and dining-room while we've nought else to do. Come on, and stir yourself. Waiting puts years on a body. Let's be busying ourselves.'

Work was an anodyne. Scrubbing floors, dusting walls, washing covers, and curtains, drying them by the kitchen fire, without time to think about Mark or worry about the telephone, which never stopped ringing, but was never the call they wanted. Everyone in the village had heard about Mark, and was concerned. Ned came up, bringing Sable, who settled down with the other animals in front of the fire, enjoying warmth and company. He was used to Deedee and Candy, as he trained with them three times a week. Rusty sometimes came too, but the little fox had no notion of obedience, and usually had to be shut in the kitchen, where he cried to join in. Candy adored Sable, and tucked herself between his paws, and he licked her nose. She was too young for serious training, but she liked to watch, and to follow, and try and copy the older dogs.

'You'll have an Alsatian-beagle cross one fine day, if you don't watch that pair,' Joe said. He had an aptitude for caricature and was entertaining Susie by drawing the animals, putting clothes on them, humanizing them.

John Linney called, worried about Sheila, and was glad to find her busy. Bess was a godsend. Her rough tongue might scar, but her ways in a crisis were always down to earth and sensible. Bess herself, coming out to empty her bucket and fetch clean water, looked at the doctor.

'It's bad, isn't it?' she said.

John Linney nodded. He had rung the hospital that morning. Mark was on the danger list. They had operated as soon as he arrived. Sheila ought to be beside him, but there was no way of getting her there. The helicopter was busy, and there was sickness on the fells. A shepherd had been flown off to hospital an hour before, suffering from pneumonia. He had carried on too long, although he had flu. He was anxious about his sheep. And every part of England was suffering from the snowfall. Men were stretched beyond endurance, struggling against the climate. No help from anywhere else was remotely possible.

Dai, driven to desperation, went out to groom Conker. The old horse was delighted to see him, but there was a listlessness about the animal that Dai did not like. Susie, coming to talk to her father, stroked the horse's neck.

'He's never very hungry in the winter,' she commented. 'He hasn't eaten at all today, Daddy.'

Dai went on brushing. He tried to estimate Conker's age. Lysbeth had sold him to Dai for Mollie. How many years ago? Mollie had been six. Nearly fourteen years ago, and Conker was twelve when they bought him. Lysbeth had bred and schooled him, and he was gentle as a sleeping kitten. Twenty-six years. He frowned at his small daughter.

'I thought he was feeding well,' he said. He rarely had time for his own animals, unless Sheila reported that they were ill. It was weeks since he had handled Conker.

'He doesn't eat much,' Susie said again. 'When's Mark coming home? Why did he go away, Daddy? Tim said he went in the helicopter.'

'He's just had to go to hospital for a little while,' Dai said, hoping it was true.

'I wish I'd gone in the helicopter. Mark has all the fun. It isn't fair.'

She ran off again, leaving Dai standing beside Conker. How had it happened? He never noticed anything about his own family. He was always rushing off to someone else's sick beast, miles away. Guilt settled on him, clouding his thoughts, and he could not move. Michael, coming out to say lunch was ready, thought that all the world congregated in the stable. He wanted to tell Dai he was sorry, that Mark would be all right, that he would like to stay on as assistant, and hoped they would not send him away now that the need for a locum was ended, that he was as miserable as they, but he said nothing. Words were futile.

'Have a look at Conker,' Dai said. 'Susie says he's not eating. Why didn't anyone tell me?'

Michael stared at him, and then walked over to the horse. He had thought, two days before, that Conker was showing his age, and was gaunt. The hollows on his head were deep, and his ribs were visible. Michael slid his hands over the smooth hide, and a moment later they told him the answer. The lump in the horse's belly was hard and heavy and only too easy to feel.

'Cancer,' he said, and Dai nodded. It was all that he needed to complete his personal hell, and he would have to tell Susie. And Mollie. And he would have to fetch his gun.

'Shall I do it, or shall we wait?' Michael asked. He didn't want to. It was something he could not bear. No one could calmly destroy an animal that had played an integral part in his own life. Dai shook his head.

'Better get it done. Thinking makes it worse. And he, at least, won't know anything about it.' Dai walked out of the stable door. 'He trusts me, and he won't be afraid of me. He might be afraid if he sees you with a gun. I don't think he knows about guns, but you can never be sure.'

There were paths dug through the snow, to coachhouse and stable, to barn and to paddock. Michael, leading the old horse to the field that afternoon, felt like a traitor, especially when Conker, delighted to be free from his loose box, rubbed a friendly nose against Michael's shoulder. Dai, following, noticed and said nothing. He swallowed, positioned himself, and aimed.

The gun spoke once.

Michael and Ned and Tim dug away in the snow in the orchard in silence, preparing the ground. Dai had telephoned to Mollie, who had asked that Conker might be buried with their other animals. She could not bear the thought of his carcase being sold for dog meat. Her voice had been desolate.

Dai walked away, remembering the look in the horse's eyes as he fell. A vet shouldn't keep animals of his own, but that was daft. You might as well say a doctor shouldn't have children. They all did. And one always got involved with a household pet, in the end. Conker had been part of their lives for fourteen years; he was older than Mark and Susie and had given rides to all the children. Mollie had won rosettes with him in the local Shows. The proud red colours decorated the beam in the stable. The old horse had come to greet them when they visited him; had played idiotic games of Chase-me-Charlie with the dogs; had rubbed his nose confidingly against Dai's face.

Dai whistled the animals. They came running, a small procession, and he led them to the orchard. It seemed cruel, but it would save the heartbreak of watching them hunt fruitlessly for a mysteriously vanished companion. He watched them nose the dead horse, saw the tails go down and the heads turn to him.

They watched the dark earth cover the dead body, and followed Dai back to the house, all of them subdued. They would recover within a few hours, and there would be no aimless searching. They knew that Conker had left them, and could never return.

Ned met Dai as he walked heavily back to the house, and took the gun and cleaned it, knowing how the vet felt. Ned had been fond of Conker too, and he was as worried as Dai and Sheila about Mark. Poor little lad. Life wasn't fair.

The House of Beasts was silent that night except for Susie. No one could stop her tears. Conker had gone. Her darling, lovely Conker. He shouldn't have had to die. God was wicked. She hated God and she hated Dai. He had killed the horse. She would not be comforted. She would not go to bed. She would not eat, and when John Linney called in to say there was still no good news about Mark, he gave her a sedative. Susie's grief was always a problem. She was as passionate as Mark. Bess, who had stayed to cook supper before struggling back along the icy village street, took the child upstairs. Sheila was exhausted, her face white, her eyes enormous.

'Has Mark a chance?' she forced herself to ask John.

She had to know.

'About fifty fifty.' John Linney, in his turn, had to be honest. It had taken time, precious time, to get the boy to hospital. He went out, wishing he could have been more reassuring, but it was useless to raise false hopes. Joe joined Ned in the yard.

'I ought to go somewhere else,' he said. 'I'm in the way.'

'You can come back with Bess or me,' Ned answered. 'But, honest, I think you're best here. It gives them some distraction, and you're a help with Susie, poor little weasel. God knows what she'll be like tomorrow.'

'God help them all if her brother dies,' Joe said. He stared up at the sky, which was dark with sullen cloud. 'Makes you think, something like this. There are times when I wish I had no kids. They're a pest. But . . . mister, am I glad I've got them.'

'You stay glad,' Ned said soberly. 'I never missed them when I was young, but in old age it hits hard. It's lonely without kids.'

He whistled to Sable, and went down the snow-banked drive to the village street, which had been cleared by the plough and was now slushy, with ice beneath the surface making it more treacherous than ever. The church bulked high against the night.

Ned was not a religious man, and he did not care for churches. God, he thought, was a power, a presence, there in the fields and on the fells and on the mountains, but meaningless in the stifling dusty buildings built to cage Him.

Yet, on an impulse, he went inside, and the Vicar, arriving to lock up, found the old man kneeling at the altar, in the eerie gloom, moonbeams ghosting round his head, Sable lying quiet beside him. The Vicar, knowing why he was there, knelt down and joined him. Mark belonged to all of them, if only God would spare him. It was a long time before either man rose from his knees.

CHAPTER SIXTEEN

THREE days of misery passed before they knew Mark was out of danger. Three days in which life had only a semblance of normality. Few animals could be brought to the surgery, and Dai could only advise the farms and stables by telephone. He hoped the diphtheria had not spread to the other calves at Throcken End. He rang Lysbeth. She had bad news about Steve, who seemed determined not to recover. Lysbeth was shocked to hear about Mark and sad to hear about Conker.

Joe, still unable to retrieve his lorry, or even reach his home, helped with the animals. Susie was quieter, but a visit to the empty stable to look for Elliott produced another storm of sobs. Tim, defeated by the situation, developed a desperate cheerfulness that irritated everybody. Tim's reactions in emergencies were often trying. Tim himself was exasperated. He was neither child nor adult, but somewhere in between, and badly frightened by the suddenness with which illness could strike. He had seen Mark as they carried him out, and had been sure his brother was dying. Human death was unimaginable. He lay awake at night, and darkness gripped his throat, so that he had to switch on a light to keep nightmare at bay. Michael, seeing the light shine across the snow, went down to talk to Tim, and they joined Joe, who, also unable to sleep, had gone quietly downstairs and made a pot of tea. Both Dai and Sheila had taken sleeping tablets prescribed by John Linney. The house itself brooded uncomfortably and the animals were all subdued.

It was Tim, answering the telephone next day, who first heard that Mark was off the danger list, and recovering, and there was no need for further worry. His yell startled Sheila, who was cleaning the kennels.

'Mum! He's O.K. Mark's O.K.'

Deedee, startled, butted Tim and tumbled him into the snow. She was a powerful animal. Sheila's legs no longer belonged to her. She leaned against the rough wooden wall, shaken by tears, and Michael, seeing her, recognizing reaction, helped her into the house. Bess produced strong tea and a glass of brandy and packed Sheila off to bed.

That night, the thaw began, and with the thaw came callers. Three days later, Mark received such a large mail that his bedside table was piled high, and he wondered if he would be able to read everything before he went home.

Ned sent a newsy letter about his three S's. Tim wrote a bumper effort. Mollie wrote a comic poem about Mark's ride in the helicopter, and Susie sent a drawing. Michael composed an illustrated letter supposed to have been written by the animals, with Deedee's pawmark, and Elliott's teethmarks, five hairs from Sim's and Rusty's tails, and a lick from Candy, which was entirely accidental and made the ink run. He added a caricature of Tia chasing a mouse. Mark, reading it, thought it was almost worth being ill.

Joe went. The thaw quickened when a warm wind, blowing from the South, melted the snow rapidly and brought fresh misery. Water lay round Sheerlings; water backed up towards Deep Willows; water clawed with chilly slap and suck and swirl at many cottage walls. Ice skimmed its surface. The valley was gone. Swans rode down the village street; ducks swam where cattle normally grazed; and Michael, waking, unaware that floods could come with such speed, looked out of his window, appalled.

Dai, two hours later, driving along the high road over the fells, to see if he could reach Throcken End, felt defeated. Perhaps the valley should be flooded permanently after all. Life was total misery. He passed Sheerlings, lying a hundred feet below him. The water had not yet reached the farmhouse. It stood, centuries old, a part of history. There had always been Wellans at Sheerlings. He drove on.

Throcken End was above the encroaching flood, but lay sodden and sullen under dirty snow that had not yet melted. Ella Grey met him, smiling, and Dai was startled, realizing that she had once been very pretty, and was not as old as she looked. Life had used her ill. She led him to the calf pen. Dai guessed, from her manner, what he would find.

The three little beasts that looked up at him might never

115

have been ill. They were beginning to thrive and one small heifer calf butted another, frisky with life.

'The last one's not doing,' Ella said. 'I didn't expect to save three, though, so I mustn't grumble.' She had salvaged seventy-five per cent of her outlay, Dai thought. He looked at the fourth calf. It was almost moribund. He gave it a quick and merciful death. Ella presented him with another dozen eggs and a promise. Jack was busy, working on the cowshed, as the contractors were still missing. The hammer blows echoed relentlessly as he drove the nails home.

Dai's next call was to the riding stables. He had to take the longest road, but Michael was on duty at the House of Beasts, and Dai was worried about Mollie. His anxiety was eased when she ran to meet him, and greeted him with a quick hug.

'I thought you'd never get through,' she said.

'Time you came home for a rest,' Dai told her.

She nodded.

'I wish I'd been home when Mark was first taken ill. I could have helped Mum.' She, too, had been frightened when she had heard the news.

'We're almost back to normal now.' Dai looked round the stables. The rugged horses looked fit again. Only two were coughing, and the mare with pneumonia was also mending. She greeted Dai with a snort. He held out his hand, and she dropped her tongue into it, and he grinned and shook the long fleshy lump that rested trustingly in his palm. It was an absurd habit that had started long ago. As he moved away her head came forward to nuzzle his face.

'She's a nice old thing,' Mollie said affectionately.

Dai went indoors to talk to the owners while Mollie fetched her coat.

'Not much doing this weather,' Jake Barrat observed. He sighed. The stable takings were always badly down in such weather.

Dai nodded.

'It's just as well,' Jake went on. 'We couldn't have given any rides. I don't think a single horse missed the epidemic. Don't know what we'd have done without your Mollie. You want to keep an eye on her. She gets so obsessed with sick horses that she won't stop to eat. We've been right bothered about her.'

Some minutes later Mollie, sitting in the Land-Rover beside her father, looked out over the fells.

'It seems ages since I was home,' she said. 'I'm going to miss Conker.'

'It's long enough.' Dai did not want to remember Conker's reproachful eyes. He stopped the engine, and they looked at the spread of water that covered the fields below them. There lay fear, realized.

'I don't know,' he said at last. 'Maybe it would be better if they did flood the place for good.'

'And leave us where?' Mollie asked.

He had no answer. Steve Johns had come home from hospital the day before the floods started. Steve, who was only a memory of himself, spent all his time sitting forlorn in his chair, huddled by the fire, never answering when Lysbeth spoke. Lysbeth, working round the farm, was grim and un-smiling. Mollie, who had telephoned several times to ask about her godfather, had been shocked by her godmother's bitterness. There was no longer any pleasure at Deep Willows.

Wind dried the water, and Mark came home. Wind blew over the fells. March hastened after February, full of bluster. Michael, now part of the household permanently, and officially Dai's assistant, could not believe his luck. He had fallen on a clover patch. He was welcomed as part of the family, he had his own quarters, as it was easier if he lived on the premises, and he fitted in easily, as if he had always belonged.

Sheila offered him three of the attics, if he liked to clean them and convert them himself, and he leaped at the opportunity. Tim enthusiastically wielded paint brushes, while Mark watched and offered advice that was seldom accepted, and Michael made himself a modern suite of rooms, of which he was immensely proud. Here he could be alone if he wished, but, more often than not, Mark came up to do his homework and listen to records, and Tim and the dogs sprawled on the big window seat, and Susie came to draw.

Mark tired easily, but had recovered remarkably well from his ordeal. His main regret was that he had been too ill to remember the helicopter flight, and had returned by car. Sheila drove to Bradford to collect him. His experience had given him a new importance at school. His class-mates were envious.

Elliott adopted Michael, and slept on his bed, and Candy romped upstairs to call him every morning. And Mollie was there, talking endlessly about horses. She came home late at night, and sat for a brief hour, before going wearily to bed. Michael made a habit of going to meet her.

Life settled into a semblance of normality. Term ended before an early Easter. Lambing would soon begin on the fells. Michael and Dai were busy, but life was manageable until one morning they received an agonized call from Dougal Hamilton's wife. Dougal, examining a stallion at a stable on the other side of the county, had been kicked and was in hospital with a broken leg, and rib injuries. She had failed to find a locum and could Dai help. Dougal's practice was not so far flung as Dai's, and another vet, on the other side of the county, had promised to deal with the small animals. But there were several farms, and two breeding studs, as well as the stables that Dai had visited at Christmas.

It doubled the work and the length of many journeys, but there was no choice. There was never any choice. Dai was soon trying to find a foster mare to feed an orphaned foal, and, within hours of the phone call there was another baby animal for Sheila to hand rear. Sheila accepted the little filly foal with pleasure. There had been a great gap since Conker had gone and it was good to have an occupant in the stables again. Deedee, certain that the newcomer needed mothering, slept with her, and kept her warm and contented. Soon the foal was running to Sheila whenever she saw her, sure that food was due again. Susie haunted the stables, adoring the foal.

It was Susie's yell, a few mornings later, that alerted all of them.

'Look at Elliott!'

Elliott, now almost full grown, was walking sedately up the drive, carrying something in his mouth that struggled violently.

Susie wailed.

'He's caught a baby squirrel.'

Sheila ran to Elliott who dropped his trophy and stood above it. Sheila stared. It was not a squirrel. It was a tiny ginger kitten, and only one eye was half open. It could not yet be ten days old.

'Oh, Elliott,' she said. 'What have you done?'

She took the kitten indoors. She would have to find out where it belonged. She hoped Elliott was not going to make a habit of bringing such tropies home. Meanwhile, the kitten constituted another problem. She sat at the table, feeding it with milk from a medicine dropper. When she had finished Candy came to her, nosed her gently, and, a moment later, took the kitten with delicate jaws and returned it to the hearthrug. She settled herself, and the kitten snuggled against the beagle, and went to sleep. The little creature remained a total mystery. Nobody knew where he came from except Elliott, and he couldn't speak. Meanwhile Candy and Sheila between them acted as foster mothers.

March ended. April came, wild and wet and windy, and lambing began. Dai and Michael spent hours on the fells, sometimes operating in mud, wind vicious on hands and faces, rain trickling down their necks. Sometimes they operated in comfort, but farms where there were lambing parlours were still rare. Dai performed a Caesarian at Pete Lanark's, in a shed that had been scrubbed and cleaned and lined with straw. He performed another at a farm further down the valley on a makeshift table that gave way at the slightest awkward movement. Michael, who was with him, sat beneath the table, holding it still, while Dai removed the lamb. The ewe was dead, and they went home with yet another mouth for the House of Beasts to feed, as the farmer was short-handed and already bottle-rearing six lambs. His ewes were given to producing twins, but, on such poor land, could rarely find enough milk to feed two.

Spring was lambing, nothing but lambing, and Michael, busier than ever before, could think only of sheep. He smelled of sheep, he tasted sheep, he was never away from sheep, and when Sheila unthinkingly produced lamb for lunch, he couldn't eat it. She promised to steer clear in future. Whatever he did, Michael thought, he would never count sheep in an effort to woo sleep. Not that effort was needed, as when he eventually got to his bed he dropped as though pole-axed, and nothing woke him. Dai had to shake him each morning, and he stumbled down to breakfast as if he were sleep-walking.

The stallion at Trapperton ran a temperature, and Dai called at the stables, as Kurt feared flu, but luckily it was only a cold, and cleared without complications. Beowulf began to recognize Dai, and greeted him by whickering whenever he heard the vet's voice. On his last visit to the stables the telephone rang as he was leaving the stallion's loose box, and a tiny boy summoned him to answer it.

He was a slender child, looking little older than Mark.

'Peter want to be a jockey,' Kurt said, smiling at the boy. 'He is small enough, eh?'

Dai looked at the boy, in his turn, and smiled and nodded before going to the telephone. Jerry Howarth, the owner of a big intensive cattle farm beyond Gallows End, was on the line.

'Thank God you're close,' he said. 'I think we've got foot and mouth here. For heaven's sake come right over.'

Dai put the receiver back in the cradlle and went outside, his face bleak. Jerry Howarth at Colliedown House had four hundred cows and the Lord alone knew how many sheep and pigs. It was the biggest farm for miles. Men from almost every county came to visit and admire and absorb new ideas. The cattle, during the winter, lived in airy spacious buildings where they had ample exercise walking through a maze that led to automated feeders. A fleet of lads cleaned up four times a day. In summer the animals were pastured in roomy paddocks.

Each cow knew her own stall, above which was her name, a little of her history, and the prize-winning rosettes she had gained at the Shows. If Colliedown got foot and mouth . . .

Dai drove the Land-Rover at breakneck speed over the narrow road to Gallows End, changed down savagely on the hill, and slowed for the bend in the road, mentally going over the routine, the symptoms and the necessary procedure. Notifying the police. Standstill orders. Slaughter. He remembered the epidemic of '67 and felt sick. Not again, dear God, not again. All the little farms in his area were at risk.

He skidded to a halt, brakes screeching. Jerry hurried to meet him. Jerry was small, his dapper little body invariably dressed in cream-coloured breeches and a hacking jacket, his immaculate boots gleaming. Wavy dark hair thrust up from his head, defying brush and comb. His dark moustache was neatly trimmed, his brown face seamed and lined. Rumours said that in spite of his dark hair the farmer was well over seventy. He stared at Dai, wanting a miracle, his eyes as beseeching as a dog's. Hell, Dai thought. Hell. Hell. Hell.

'Where is she?' he asked, speaking much more abruptly than he had intended.

'As far away as I could get her and a fat lot of use that is,' Jerry said miserably.

'When did you notice she was ill?'

'That's what's so odd,' Jerry answered. 'She hasn't been off her food. She's been as frisky as you please. But for the last hour she's been like a mad thing, frothing at the mouth. I can't understand how we could have failed to notice.'

The sick beast was a young heifer calf, sleek red and white. Dai looked at her, noting the froth round her jaws. She stared at him, wild-eyed. Her coat was shining with health, burnished as if it had been polished. He frowned at her, bewildered.

'God knows what's wrong, but it's not foot and mouth,' he said roughly, his voice harsh with relief. He walked over to the calf and opened her jaws. 'It's crazy. What's she had to eat?'

'Nothing out of the way, so far as I know,' Jerry said.

Dai wiped his hand over the heifer's lips. They were slimy. He bent to examine her more closely, and she flung up her head, slapping his own lips with her tongue.

'Soap, by God,' he exclaimed. 'She's been eating soap.'

Jerry stared at him, electrified. He ran to the door of the cow byre, and called to a boy who was standing near.

'I want all of you. At once. ' His tone was ominous. The boy cast a startled look at him, and ran. Within minutes eight men were lined up, joined by two lads in their teens.

'Who fed the calves?' Jerry asked.

There was no answer. The farmer glared and one of the boys moved forward, his face scarlet, his eyes appalled.

'Tansy's been eating soap. How did she get it?' Jerry's voice was vicious with anger.

The boy stared up at him, unable to reply.

There was a sudden yell from the house. A small, grey-haired woman, red-faced, and plumper than a Christmas goose, waddled militantly towards them.

' 'oo's pinched me bucket?' she demanded.

'Did you?' Jerry asked the boy.

He nodded.

'Did you clean it before you put in the milk?'

The boy shook his head.

'I didn't put any milk in when I saw it was dirty,' he said. 'I took the bucket by mistake. She'd put it down beside ours. I put it in the calf shed. I meant to take it back when I got time. And then Tansy shuffled in it and ate the soap. She'll eat anything. I didn't dare tell,' he finished miserably. 'I thought mebbe it wouldn't hurt her.'

'Take him away and shoot him,' Jerry said to the farm manager, who joined them at that moment, seeing the group. 'The calf's eaten soap. It's not foot and mouth at all, Hilton.'

The farm manager, an impressive man in his middle years, had grey hair which was turning white. His brown eyes sparked with sudden anger.

'Shooting's too good for him. I'll turn him into pigmeal,' he said. 'I've just about given myself an ulcer in the last hour, worrying about an epidemic. Saw all my cattle dead, and all of us out of a job. I'm glad I'm not in your shoes, son. Come on.' He ended abruptly.

The boy's face was white as he followed the man across the yard.

'What is it, Tilly?' Jerry asked, as the little woman stood her ground, staring at him, reminding Dai of Elliott's expression when he wanted food, or water, or out, and no one heeded him.

'I've lost me piece of soap, that's what it is, and somebody had better find me another. I left me soap in me bucket. 'Ow can I clean up without soap? Somebody's light-fingered round 'ere, I can tell yer that. Can't leave a bucket around for a minute but somebody pinches it, and that was a nice new bit o' soap.'

The men, about to disperse, were grinning, and Dai suddenly realized that the woman was deaf, and had not heard a word of the argument.

'I'll give you some soap, Tilly,' one of the men said, as Jerry was reduced to speechlessness. They walked away, while the rest of the men resumed their jobs. Dai went back to look at the calf. It would come to no lasting harm, and there was certainly no epidemic.

'I don't want that kind of soap.' Tilly's voice rose high at the other end of the yard. 'I want a nice bit of carbolic and maybe that'll stop folk swiping it from me.'

'I'm glad that bit wasn't carbolic,' Jerry said. He filled a bucket with water and gave it to the calf to drink. 'Soap! Soap! I ask you.' He put down the bucket and Dai began to laugh and a moment later Jerry joined in.

'Come and have some coffee and celebrate.' Jerry was exultant with relief and Dai followed him into the house, admiring the antiques with which Mary Howarth had filled the place when she came to it, almost half a century ago, as a bride.

Dai had never visited Colliedown House before. Mary, small, fragile and white-haired, rose from her chair to pour the coffee, moving slowly, with extreme difficulty, refusing to acknowledge the arthritis that had claimed her as a victim.

'What was wrong with the calf, Jerry?' she asked, well aware from her husband's demeanour that it was not disaster.

'One of those lazy little louts took Tilly's bucket and left it in the calf shed. Tansy had a bellyful of soap,' Jerry said.

Mary Howarth stared at him.

'Thank God that's all it was. I was so worried. I saw all our work wasted. All those years.'

'We were all worried,' Jerry said. 'Little fool. If you weren't here, I'd say something strong. I thought we'd had it, for sure.'

Hilton came into the room and took the cup that Mary handed to him.

'He'll never do that again. Right now he's wishing he'd never been born. I'll give him one more chance,' the manager said. 'That lad's a pest. He's too lazy to live. God! I was scared sick.'

Tilly put her head round the door.

'Please, Ma'am,' she said, 'I dunno where I put me soap. It's got legs on it today, that soap 'as. Can I have another bit?'

'Like a lot of idyuts they were,' she told her husband that night, filled with indignation. 'I don't see nothing to laugh at in a cake of soap.'

Dai, writing up his records just before midnight, grinned to himself at the memory, and Michael, who was playing with Candy and teaching her to come to her name, looked up at him.

'Something funny?' he asked. He had been out to a late call to help a mare whose foal was caught at the hips. He had been successful and was jubilant.

'Had a soapy calf this morning,' Dai said.

He stood up, nodding good night, leaving his assistant staring, convinced that the events of the last few months had finally driven his employer out of his mind.

CHAPTER SEVENTEEN

By the end of April the Dog Obedience Club was officially launched, meeting every Tuesday in the Church Hall. Ned was chief handler, and Sheila secretary, and Michael, whenever he was free, called in to help, and had to steel himself against cunning owners who tried to cadge free advice.

The hearing about the proposed reservoir had taken place late in February. At last the decision came through. The planners would not change their minds. There was to be an appeal, and Sheila, in any spare time she had, was working furiously, with the Vicar's help. Dai and Michael were aware of the phone calls and committee meetings, of a frantic busyness that occupied everyone but them, but were far too busy themselves to make inquiries.

Dai, thankful that Mark was well again, tried to make more time to spend with the children. Tim, working hard for his examinations, only a few weeks off, was touchy as a dog with a bone, snapping at everyone. He wanted to be a vet, too, and had been horrified, looking through Michael's books, to see what was entailed.

Anatomy, Histology, Physiology, Pharmacology. Care of pigs and sheep and horses and cows and chickens, and hens and geese and turkeys, all different, all with different diseases, all with different kinds of body. A doctor only had to learn about the human animal. A vet had to know something about more animals than Tim realized existed. A doctor never had to treat a falcon, or a tiger or a kangaroo. Supposing you were called into a circus, or a Zoo? You use your wits, Michael said, when asked. He was taking Mollie out for the first time, dressing himself meticulously, shaving, and putting on a new tie, anxious to make an impression.

'Honestly,' Tim said, watching. 'Anyone'd think you were in love. It's only Mollie.'

Michael, walking downstairs, grinned to himself. Tim could never imagine that his sister was attractive. Dai, looking at his assistant as he ran out into the garden, whistling, lifted an eyebrow, and went into the kitchen.

'Seen how the wind blows?' he asked Sheila, who was writing at the kitchen table. Dai watched his daughter run past the window to Michael's battered Land-Rover, which was even older than Dai's. Mollie laughed, and Michael, leaning over from the driver's seat, held out a hand to pull her in.

'A long time ago. I don't know how Mollie feels, though,' Sheila said calmly. 'I'm going out too. Bess will give you your supper.'

Dai ate alone. It was luxury to sit and eat in silence and no longer have to listen to chatter. He was very tired.

He moved away from the table, leaving the dishes, and sat by the fire. The house was quiet. There seemed to be an animal asleep in every corner and under every chair, exhausted by playing. Deedee put her head on Dai's knee and gazed at him soulfully, and Elliott, jealous, jumped on to his chair, and sat on his shoulder, and purred noisily, and the kitten, now named Toffee, jumped on to Dai's knee. Susie had been promised Toffee for her 'very own'. The child had never quite forgiven her father for Conker's death, even though she knew that Conker had been very ill.

'Mark was very ill too,' she said. 'No one shot him.'

Dai gave up. It was useless trying to explain. She would learn as she grew older. Meanwhile she remained a major problem in a house where death came visiting too often, as not all patients survived.

Michael was never quite sure whether May was heightened by his growing awareness of Mollie, or if, always, spring on the fells was total miracle. The icy winds died, and a warm breeze stroked the new-growing heather. The ground was softened by curled bracken, a smoke of new leaves masked every bush and twig, and the few trees were fuzzy with buds soft as kittens' fur.

Alternate evenings were free. He met Mollie's bus, or drove to the stables and collected her, and before bed, walked by a river that had forgotten winter fierceness, gently rippling water playing hide-and-seek with the rocks. One night an otter came to drink, two cubs behind her; another night four fox cubs played Chase-me-Charlie under the stars, tumbling over one another, snapping in excitement, until the vixen, sniffing the air, caught an alien human scent, and drove them away from imagined danger. The House of Beasts was only a step from the fells, and, when the moon shone, the wide sweep of rolling land lay before them, patched by the lights of distant farms.

One Sunday in the middle of May Michael insisted that Dai went right away from the House of Beasts. Dai tended to forget he now had an able assistant, and worried lest a call came when he was not there. But, if he walked on the fells with Mark and Ned, Tim could find him if need arose. Sheila was busy, and glad to see him go. He so rarely relaxed properly.

No expedition could be undertaken without the dogs, and Rusty. Deedee, Sable and Candy frisked in front of them. Sable was never far from Ned. He ran with the other dogs, but came back to butt Ned's hand, asking for reassurance, and twice, to stand on hindlegs and lick his master's face. It was the only sign left of his unhappy puppyhood. Rusty walked with them. Dai kept the fox leashed, and he followed at heel, dog-like.

The sun was a benison, the first hot day of the year. Ned and Dai sat by the river, while Mark paddled in the shallows. Dai looked over the valley. Winter was gone, its misery a half-forgotten memory. Here was peace, blue sky flaked with feather clouds, and a shallow stream trickling peacefully, sunlight stippling racing ripples. Overhead a lark spiralled, its song languishing on the air. A sparrow-hawk prospected from a lightning-scarred tree, thrusting into the sky on the slope beyond the water. The distant flocks of Sheerlings grazed, lambs racing among the ewes, their far-away plaint a lullaby, soothing the senses. Ned, sitting quiet, contemplating, was the perfect companion, never needing words to smooth scarred silences.

Deedee came to lie beside Dai, panting. She was frisky with summer and foolish with fun. She thrust her head at him, growling softly, begging him to run with her, to play with her, to romp on the grass, and he stood up, throwing down his jacket, and held a smooth stick out to her. Within moments Candy had joined in the game and he was chasing breathlessly, throwing sticks for all of them to retrieve, while Sable watched. All the Alsatian needed was Ned, and Ned was sitting quietly, smiling. Rusty lay beside him, ears pricked, eyes wistful. He was never allowed to run free outside the grounds of the House of Beasts. Ned fondled the fox's prick ears and Rusty made a throaty growl that was almost a purr.

The fox was full grown, and more splendid than any wild animal, as he was better fed than any beast hunting for himself. His eyes were brilliant with health, his ears alert for every sound, and from his magnificent ruff to his bushy brush he was breath-taking.

Ned scratched the fox gently behind one ear. Rusty, who counted Ned as family, turned and nibbled the brown finger, his mouth gentle, bestowing a caress. Ned wondered what the fox made of life; whether he truly believed he was as much a dog as Deedee or Sable; or whether, when the wind blew strong and the nights were wild, he ran to the kitchen window and stared at the misty dark, the urge to hunt rabbit and hare strong in him. Certainly he knew how to kill. He and Sim depleted the hordes of rats daily.

Ned, like Dai, hated keeping wild beasts caged, but at times there was no other choice. He sighed. People were strange. They would criticize things they knew nothing about. Like fox hunting. Yet foxes bred too freely and had to be kept down. Guns maimed and traps were slow torment, and gas a choking cruelty causing immense suffering. The Hunt's end was quick, and a fox that killed daily for his own needs well knew when he, in his turn, was running for his life, and knew too that he could escape if he were wily and wise. And he often did escape.

'Stop putting the world to rights, Ned. Today's a holiday,' Dai said lazily. He could guess the old countryman's thoughts. Ned grinned, and lay back in the grass. Rusty crept into the hollow of his arm, and watched the dogs romp, his eyes wistful. Sable put a proprietary paw on Ned's leg. He never left his master.

Dai was out of breath long before the dogs tired. He dropped to the ground, panting. Rusty wanted to run. He pawed at Mark, his fox bark sharp and yelping. Mark, who had been lying flat, basking in the sun, sat up, laughing, and pushed the hair away from his eyes.

'Can I let him run, Dad?' he asked.

Dai shook his head. It was a rule that must never be broken. Rusty was a fox and not a dog. He did not always come when called, and he was a great rat hunter. He knew how to kill. There was no guarantee that he might not chase after sheep, given the chance. He was a wild animal with wild instincts and Dai had no idea at all whether domestication might overlay them.

He felt he must take every precaution, and not give the fox the chance to revert to type. He had brought him up in a house, and he owed it to the little beast to protect him against his own instincts if necessary.

'Can he run on Sable's training leash?' Ned asked.

He was teaching the Alsatian to track, and he kept a special long-running harness for him, based on the police dog tracking harness. The leash lay by his side now, neatly coiled.

'I don't see why not.'

Dai yawned lazily. They were alone, and had seen no one all day. The fells stretched around them, limitless, the horizon bounded by distant peaks. Remote, far away, toy houses in a toy landscape, lay Sheerlings and Deep Willows and the House of Beasts. Tiny people walked along the road below them, and tiny cars raced over a tiny bridge. It was a landscape from a fairy story and they were giants in Lilliput. They were the only reality in an unreal world.

Rusty raced ahead of Mark, his fox face eager. Deedee ran behind, gambolling absurdly, falling over her legs, chasing her tail. Freedom was rare, and she was making the most of it. Dai leaned his chin on his hands and watched the boy and the dogs and the fox. This was the way one should live, not cooped up in concrete cities in which people lost their souls and starved through the years to slow death, deprived of trees and flowers, of lakes and hills, of woods and rolling fells, of freedom and beauty.

Dai's thoughts were interrupted by a sudden yell.

Deedee barked and Sable sprang, and growled viciously, and Mark flung himself headlong on top of Rusty who turned and snapped, terrified by the sudden, bewildering and unexpected onslaught. The shot that had been fired ploughed into the ground, missing Mark by a fraction of an inch. A moment later there was a throaty roar, a bellow of pain, and Brook Holler came racing towards Dai, Deedee barking savagely at his heels, and Sable leaping at his throat. Dai shouted, and the dogs barked again, and then, as Ned signalled to them, backed away, growling ferociously.

Mark was shaking. Dai ran to him and discovered that the shot had grazed a shallow furrow across the boy's thigh, and Rusty's teeth had bitten deep in his fright. Dai picked up the gun, which the man had dropped when the dogs ran at him, and broke it open, and made sure it was empty. He laid it on the ground, took a stone, and hammered it until it was beyond repair.

'Try suing me for that,' he said. 'Just try.'

It was a bad end to the day. Dai was grim-faced as they walked down the hill. The dogs walked behind Brook Holler, Sable ready and anxious to snatch a bite if the man moved out of line. None of the three dogs had used their teeth. Candy was behind, her own eyes eager, watching the man. Ned poked Brook Holler in the back with the barrel of the wrecked gun and Sable barked. Mark walked proudly beside Dai, the pain in his leg masked by the thought that no other boy he knew had ever been shot. And he'd saved Rusty, by throwing him out of the line of fire, even if the poor little beast had bitten him.

'O.K., son?' Dai asked anxiously. There was murder in his heart. Both fists were clenched, deep in his pockets, and he dared not speak to Brook. He remembered the threat made on the moors some weeks before. What had the man said? 'If I see that fox outside the House of Beasts ...' Damn the stupid bastard. A man with children could not afford enemies like Holler.

Mark nodded. He'd had worse injuries, and neither of these hurt as much as his appendix had. These were scars of glory. He could see himself at school, showing them to everyone, and the thought was heady.

The police came, and went, with Brook Holler under arrest. John Linney came to attend to Mark. Rusty lay quiet, and Dai looked at the little fox, worried. Suppose he bit again? But the situation had been unusual and terrifying. In future the fox would have to stay at home. There was no safety for him in the world outside.

The doctor went, and Dai stood at his gate, looking down to the village, at the straggling cottages that lay beside the river, at the distant farms. They must not flood the valley. Never mind snow, or flood, or winter. Never mind the difficulties. They could be overcome.

He turned and looked back at the House of Beasts, standing squarely against the wind, an old house, devoid of any architectural charm but, nevertheless, home. His family were inside, temporarily safe. Worry tugged at him. There was always fear. The afternoon's incident had been extremely nasty, and could have been much worse. Had the man intended to kill the fox? Or just to frighten, out of malice? Dai did not know. It alarmed him to think of someone lurking unseen. How did any man know what passions he aroused in others? A casual word, an off-hand remark, a slight, perhaps only imagined, could provoke fury. And he himself did more than that. He lashed out at cruelty and neglect and the men he lashed were never wholly civilized. Reasonable men did not starve, neglect, or torture animals. Dai walked indoors, feeling that even the afternoon's pleasure had exacted a price.

Take what you want, and pay for it, says God. Surely the incident with Holler had been payment enough, but all the same premonition needled him, as the sun went in, and blue sky was forgotten, replaced by sullen, lowering cloud.

The telephone, ringing at midnight, was total intrusion. Dai answered it sleepily, having gone early to bed, exhausted by the events of the afternoon. He listened, and sat up, startled, and, unusually, switched on the light, waking Sheila, who took one look at his face, and immediately jumped out of bed and put on jeans and jersey. More trouble. But what kind of trouble? Trouble, it seemed, did indeed never walk alone.

'We'll both come, right away,' Dai said, putting down the receiver.

'Ask Michael to come and sleep in my bed, beside the telephone, in case anything else happens tonight,' he said.

'What is it?' Sheila asked. She knew from his expression that it was bad.

'Steve's dead.'

It was too abrupt but Dai could not wrap it up. He began to dress, his back to Sheila to avoid talking, and his wife walked upstairs, choked by a lump in her throat, her eyes stinging. She returned within a few minutes with Michael.

'Don't hurry back,' Michael said.

'We'll bring Lysbeth with us if we can persuade her to come, even if it's only for tonight,' Dai answered, as he took the keys of the Land-Rover off his dressing-table.

The clouds had parted. A thin moon shone over the fells. The Land-Rover rattled over the road, mile after mile stretching into the distance. All around was mystery. Nothing had changed since man first came to hide in the valleys and to banish the fear-ridden dark. Others had lived here, and where were they now? And where was Steve? What was death? A beginning? An ending? Dai did not know.

Deep Willows was alive with light. Lysbeth had switched on every light in every room, as if to counteract the darkness that was death. She came to meet them, her face a carefully controlled mask. John Linney was in the kitchen, warming his hands on a cup filled with scalding coffee, staring into the fire, with nothing whatever to say. He nodded at Dai, who went into the bedroom and looked down at Steve, who lay beyond all fear, the room as quiet as he. The planners had done this, with their glib stupidity, as surely as if they had taken a knife and twisted it deep. He walked to the window, and looked at the sky. Where was God? The star above him was an isolated point in deep space, lying between drifting clouds that soon would mask the dark.

Was life, after all, a tale told by an idiot, signifying nothing?

A cold nose crept into his hand. Dai looked down. Steve's golden retriever had come to him for comfort. Bran had never, in his life, come to anyone but Steve before. Dai knelt beside the dog, unable to face the others in the kitchen. He was totally unmanned.

CHAPTER EIGHTEEN

THERE was no longer reality. Everyone was shocked by Steve's death. Sheila helped Lysbeth answer letters. Dai and Ted made all necessary arrangements. Adam came on leave from college, and sat, stony faced, in the kitchen at the House of Beasts. All his life, he had expected to inherit Deep Willows. Now he had, and 'They' were out to foil him. 'They' assumed giant proportions in his mind. He knew just how his uncle had felt. 'They' were killers. The faceless men behind the regulations. He had no comfort for his aunt, and only bitterness for himself.

Steve's funeral was the biggest gathering of the year. The sun mocked their sorrow, shining from a brilliant sky, gleaming through the glowing glass of the church windows, a transient beam lighting the Vicar's head as he read the service, his own voice rough with sadness. Steve had been a friend as well as a parishioner.

Ten days after the funeral, life was almost normal. Adam was coming to live at Deep Willows as soon as he finished college. He would farm there for what was left of its life. The appeal had not yet been heard, but no one was hopeful. In the Swan, at night, the men sat apathetic, fearing the future. All of them worked on the land, and none of them knew where they would go. Tempers flared. Men drank too much and grew morose. The women were edgy and quarrelsome.

The appeal would soon be heard. Sheila spent three days working, and went to the Vicarage with the result. She had little hope. She was not so busy now. The lambs were out at grass, and the foal, weaned, had returned to her own home.

Elliott, now a handsome full-grown cat, began to wander over the fells, where there were always mice hiding under the grasses. His eager tail, bolt upright above his body, was as expressive as his face as he watched, fascinated, the little green grasshoppers that leaped unexpectedly, making extraordinary noises, and little frogs that hopped. He had adopted the kitten, Toffee, as a brother, and played endless games with him, but Toffee did not like the wide spaces, and preferred to stay near home. The world beyond the garden was too big and frightening.

The day of the appeal came closer and tempers fractured. Everyone felt helpless. No one could fight the juggernaut that threatened them all. It was too vast, with all the power of the law behind it. It was legal murder, licensed by the Government. The villagers had to suffer so that the townsfolk could bathe and wash and drink.

Dai was alone in the kitchen when Elliott walked home carrying a small black kitten in his jaws. The kitten was almost a replica of the older cat, but that was not possible as he had been neutered and Tia had been spayed. It was three weeks old, and needed feeding. Dai looked down at it helplessly as it lay mewing at his feet. Elliott was a pest.

Elliott watched with interest, his head cocked to one side. A few minutes later he vanished again. Dai found a dropper and warmed some milk and fed the kitten. Candy cuddled it close and it tried to suck, and, defeated, fell asleep. Dai started his accounts. He was engrossed in them when Elliott yowled. There was a second black kitten on the floor.

This time, when Elliott trotted off, Dai followed. He must find the mother, and make sure the kittens were fed, or else destroy them. He could not let them starve to death. She must be living wild on the fells. Elliott walked through the gate, along the lane, and turned on to the moorland, bounding over clumped grass, his eyes intent. Dai followed the cat for over a hundred yards, to a hollow not far from the river, where Elliott vanished.

Dai walked over and looked down. There was a tiny cave, only big enough to shelter a cat. The pillared rocks round it reminded him of standing stones, but were too small. Grey, lichened, weathered, they leaned at crazy angles, the cave situated beneath one of them. Elliott came out with a third kitten in his mouth. Dai took it from him, and the cat vanished again, and brought a fourth. When that too was taken from him he turned for home, as if his task were finished. Dai watched him go, bewildered. The mother could not be far away. He was surprised that she had not attacked Elliott.

He found her a few minutes later, lying dead in long grass, her throat torn. She had died the night before, he judged. He looked down at her, a pitifully thin little creature who must have come from one of the demolished cottages. Here she had found brief sanctuary that had proved a sham. Either a stoat or a weasel had killed her, and it was a miracle that the killer had not found the kits. He went to the cave, and knelt to examine it, lest Elliott had overlooked a fifth. There Tim found him. He bent down to look, interested.

Deedee had followed too, and seeing them apparently hunting in the grass, she began to dig. Her paws tore up the turf, scratching on rock. Tim glanced down, and, a moment later, he bent down, excited. He ran to the river and, coming back, pushed his father unceremoniously aside, mopping at the ground with his soaked handkerchief. Brilliant blue glowed at them, and Michael, seeing them from a distance, came over and found them digging frantically with the bare hands, the kittens both tucked into Dai's jacket pocket. A slab of mosaic glittered in the grass, brighter than the sky.

Michael looked at the weathered rocks.

'They're pillars,' he said. He scraped the lichen, and then, more gently, used his finger nail, and bared a vein that showed marble.

'Dad!' Tim was suddenly urgent. 'I forgot. There's someone in the waiting-room.'

Dai ran. He handed the kittens to Sheila and was relieved to find that his patient was only a cat that he had promised to spay. He put her in a wire cage and went back to explain Elliott's family to Sheila. The four kittens were curled up on the hearth rug. They were pretty little creatures. The mother had fed them, and kept them clean, and they had been well cared for until her death. Susie was already making her claim, and Toffee had joined them, as he had long ago decided that Candy was his mother, and he was jealous of her attention. Dai suspected that he too was the sole survivor of some family that had laired on the hill, before being found by Elliott. He began to wonder what Elliott would bring home next.

Mark joined Tim and Michael on the fells. Tim, at Michael's insistence, ran for the Vicar, and Mark raced home to fetch Sheila. They had removed more of the encroaching turf, and discovered that the mosaic was part of a pavement. Excitement rode them, as here, it was obvious, was the remains of a Roman villa. There was only one other villa known in the whole of the Lake District. This was history, under the invading grass. This might be the most important archaeological find in years. It lay on the route the Romans used. It was known that the Romans had a fort in Cantchester. Why shouldn't a rich farmer settle here? Before long the whole family were gathered on the fells, excitement mounting.

Dai, at home once more, taking surgery, was aware of the seething house, of slamming doors and shouting voices, of the telephone in constant use. He bathed a cut paw, and gave a pup its inoculations, and cleaned an abscess on a cat's shoulder, cut a spaniel's claws, and treated a long-standing persistent eczema. The hour seemed endless, and he was desperately anxious to know what was happening. He could scarcely control his patience. A glimmer of hope had developed.

At last he finished. No one had prepared any food, even Bess having gone to see the find. Mark and Tim and Susie made toast and opened tins of sardines, as Sheila had gone off with the Vicar, to heaven knew what destination. Dai began to feel he had no wife. Michael and Mollie walked down to look at Elliott's find, and by dusk the fells were alight with the beams of torches, and alive with excited chatter, with speculation, with eager voices. Mrs. Jones, in the Swan, was busier than she had been for weeks, as everyone turned in on his way home, and an impromptu party developed.

Dai returned from the Swan, whistling. Michael had spayed the cat during the evening. She lay in her cage, stupid with anaesthetic, trying to understand why her legs betrayed her. Michael was a neat worker. Dai looked at the stitched wound, and thought that he might offer his assistant a partnership.

Sheila was standing in the kitchen, waving a bottle of sherry. The Vicar, looking strangely undressed without his dog collar, his shirt neck open, his hands brown with dirt, was toasting something, an air of delirium about him. Dai grinned, suddenly reminded of a Roman priest about to conduct a Bacchanalian orgy. The Vicar was normally a respectable Anglican cleric with an air about him that was so phlegmatic that it was painful. Susie, who ought to have been in bed, was lying, almost asleep, on the hearthrug with the kittens, Toffee curled on her lap. The dogs were sprawled on the floor, Rusty among them, his bushy brush spread out in splendour over Deedee's legs. He alone was awake, watching the crazy humans with wide astonished eyes.

Mark ran at his father, and butted him with his head. Excitement had mastered him, and he could not keep still.

'Hey, hey,' Dai said.

'You said we needed a miracle. Well, we've got one. We're sure we've got one. And all because of Elliott.'

'To Elliott! Long may he roam!' The Vicar bent to stroke the cat and laughed. 'I honestly do think we've got the answer.'

It was Sheila who, after she had undressed, struck the one sad note.

'I'm sure that this will do the trick,' she said. 'It's unique. They can't drown it, even if they can drown the valley. But it's too late for Steve. It's silly, isn't it, that we should be saved by uncovering something that was built nearly twenty centuries ago, while people who are alive today don't even matter.'

CHAPTER NINETEEN

ARCHAEOLOGISTS came to the fells. Dai, looking from his window, wondered if this would really turn the course of the appeal, and if the planners would stay their hands. It seemed ironic that a few ancient stones could affect an issue so important, while the lives of the people involved had little value. He must be growing old. He no longer liked the world he lived in. He began to agree with the poet who had written, 'Though every prospect pleases, and only man is vile.'

Dai and Michael were always busy. Often, remedying the result of men's stupidity or carelessness. They no longer had time to train their dogs, or exercise them, but they still bought them, and allowed them out to wander freely, so that in one week he and Michael operated on seven animals that had been injured in road accidents, and Sheila came home sick and shaking because a dog had run under her wheels, chasing after a cat, and she had killed it. Dai was sick of people.

He listened briefly, while Sheila told him about the progress of the research involved in setting up an appeal. Two solicitors in Cantchester were giving their services free. Both lived on the edge of the proposed new lake, which would come up to their doors. They had mustered a great many allies. A number of countrywide organizations had promised support, including those concerned with conservation. Many wild birds, and beasts, and rare plants were threatened. Now the archaeologists were involved. And an alternative site had been proposed, a far away mere, where only the hovering kestrels would have to find new homes.

The appeal, at last, was heard. Men waited, this time much more hopeful. The slow weeks passed. Nothing could be hurried. Dai and Michael worked continuously, Dai sometimes wondering if all their time was wasted time, and the farm beasts they tended were due for an untimely end, when men marched in to build the dam. Mostly, he was too busy to wonder at all.

Michael was learning fast that his life involved more than mere medicine. One day he called at a house where the child kept a pony. The animal was sick. He found it standing miserably in a stinking stables that had not been cleaned out for weeks. The hay in the net was mouldy. There was scum on the water in the filthy bucket.

Michael discovered he had a tongue as vituperative as Dai's, and he lashed at the owners. They had no right to keep any animal in such appalling conditions. He would report them to the RSPCA. He led the pony outside and persuaded it to mount a ramp into the back of the Land-Rover. It was very small, a stocky little creature with all spirit knocked out of it by harsh treatment. He took it back to the House of Beasts and led it out as Sheila was coming across the yeard.

'Oh, Michael,' she said. She looked at him despairingly. Then she laughed. 'As if Dai wasn't bad enough!'

An offer not to prosecute was sufficient to make the pony's owners surrender it to Michael, and with adequate treatment, food, fresh air, and exercise it developed into a gay little animal, amply repaying everyone for the trouble it had caused, as it had needed a great deal of nursing. When he was quite sure it was better, Michael gave it to Susie, who stared at him in total disbelief.

'Truly?' was all she could say. 'For me, truly?'

Michael, who had offered the pony during supper, nodded.

'Hurry up and marry Mollie,' Susie said. 'I do so like you.'

Mollie blushed and Michael laughed.

'I'll do just that,' he promised. 'Only Mollie hasn't said she'll have me!'

'She's not daft,' Mark said. It would be exciting to have Michael as a permanent member of the family.

'I think you could get married next week,' Susie said.

'I think that's enough and you had better go and do your homework,' Sheila said, wanting to end embarrassment for both Michael and Mollie. She wanted them to make up their minds and wished the conversation had never started.

'I've done my homework,' Susie said.

'Then just go and feed that pony of yours, and he needs

grooming too,' Michael told her. 'If you have him, you look after him, and you do it properly. Right?'

'Right,' said Susie. She ran round the table and climbed on to his knee and kissed him soundly. 'I love you nearly as much as Daddy,' she said. 'I'm going to call my pony Mike, after you.'

Michael laughed, and looked at Sheila, his face alight with mischief.

'Don't worry,' he said. 'It's all right. We aren't being pushed into anything. We've known for ages. It's just a matter of saying something. If Susie hadn't forced my hand, I don't think I'd have ever had courage.'

'We'll get married next year,' Mollie said. It was suddenly an accomplished fact, and she did not regret in the least that it had been a strange proposal. Dai, coming into the room at that moment, beamed broadly.

'I'm glad that's settled,' he said. 'Now I can settle something much more important. Michael, how about a partnership?'

Ned, walking into the room a few minutes later, was promptly overwhelmed by everyone talking at once while Mollie poured sherry. Susie was alone in the stable, grooming her pony, totally absorbed in him. She was murmuring to him, rubbing her face against his neck, telling him he was hers. She examined his hay carefully, smelling it for mustiness before stuffing it into the net.

Mollie, coming to find her and tell her the news, watched her small sister, aware that here, too, was the start of a love affair. Rusty sat by the stable door, also watching, and Mollie wondered if the little fox were jealous, but Susie had not forgotten him. She stopped brushing the pony's flowing mane and knelt in the straw and put her arms round the fox.

'I do so love them all,' she said, with total conviction. 'Isn't my pony beautiful?'

The pony, cured, well-fed, and sturdy, was beautiful. His shining bay coat contrasted with a paler mane, and his brown eyes were warmly affectionate. Life was good at the House of Beasts, and he knew it, and responded to his treatment. He revelled in attention and companionship, and there was always one animal or another with him, in field or stable, so that he was no longer lonely.

Sheila, finishing her rounds late one night, wondered why they always ended up with more beasts than they could count. The real trouble, she acknowledged ruefully to herself, as she stroked the pony before locking him in for the night, with Sim beside him in the straw, was that she was as bad as Susie. Once they had adopted any animal, even temporarily, she became attached to it.

She bolted the stable door. Elliott was weaving round her feet, and she picked him up and buried her face in his soft fur, and revelled in his delighted purr. So much had happened since Elliott first came to the House of Beasts. He had certainly been born, like Mark, under a wandering star. He explored the fells daily, and Dai swore his father had been, not a cat, but a retriever. Only the day before he had come home with a young grouse in his mouth. The grouse was quite unharmed, and later, Michael crept out, guiltily, with it hidden under his coat, and released it, feeling as if he himself had been poaching.

Sheila put the cat down, and he ran ahead of her into the kitchen. Here was sanctuary, out of the night, and she curled in the big armchair and looked down at the hearth-rug, which appeared to be teeming with animals. Rusty, as always, curled close against Elliott, and Toffee joined them. Candy always curled up with Tia. The other kittens had gone to new homes. Deedee was odd one out. Her affections were reserved for humans, and for baby animals. Dai was her life. She watched for him and waited for him, and though friendly to the rest of the family, none of them mattered if Dai were there.

Mark was busy. His project on the Romans had flared to fascinating life with the discovery of Roman remains almost on their own doorstep. The mosaic had proved to be part of a villa floor, and had been further excavated to reveal a black bull charging across a blue ground. One of the men had turned up several coins, and lent them to Mark to copy. They were smooth with age and fascinated him. He and Dai, examining them, saw visions of long-ago legionaries who had held these coins in their own hands, had paid for household goods with them, had gambled with them, had tossed them to propitiate strange gods, and had hoped that their offerings would win them safe conduct throughout life, as well as in the next.

Time was racing past. Ned and Sable were now well known

in the district, and Ned, to his huge entertainment, suddenly found himself a minor celebrity, asked to give talks about dogs and dog training to many organizations. The attendance at the Obedience Club grew, and Dai came one night to give a talk to owners. More pups were being brought to him for inoculations, and there were fewer wandering dogs in the district. Ned's work was having some effect.

Adam came to live at Deep Willows in July. Michael and Mollie announced their engagement in October, and gave a party. Michael was now a partner, and as well liked in the village as Dai. His long experience with his father, helping from childhood in the practice, had given him a way with beasts, and only now was he beginning to realize how much knowledge he had acquired during his growing years.

In the middle of the party Susie, who had been doing mysterious sums on her fingers, decided it was also Elliott's birthday and opened a tin of sardines for the cat. Tim was also celebrating as he had gained good marks in nine 'O' level subjects. He was working hard now for his higher examinations, quite determined to be a vet.

Dai left the merriment and walked to the gate. Lamplight shone on yellow leaves which drifted towards him on a sighing wind. Lysbeth and Sheila joined him. Together they looked over the valley, at the light that marked Sheerlings, at Deep Willows, at the lamps along the village street, at the greystone church, now blacker than night, hiding the colour of its weathered fabric.

Stars hung above them. Deedee came to stand beside them, indignant because they had slipped away without her knowledge. There was a darker shadow among the shadows in the garden, under the old elm tree, and as Lysbeth and Sheila walked back to seek warmth indoors, Dai walked over, and found Ned leaning against the trunk, with Sable beside him.

'We won our class in Cantchester, at the Show this afternoon,' Ned said, satisfaction in his voice. It was the realization of a long-standing ambition. He had always come second, or third, before. It took time to triumph. It took hard work, too. Nothing was ever got for nothing.

Dai went indoors. Ned followed, and the telephone rang. A calf had fallen and broken its leg at Josh's farm at Bruton. Dai left the party and drove with Ned through the dark. It was not fair to ask Michael to come. Sable waited patiently in the Land-Rover until they returned from the calf. It had been a simple break, and the little creature would recover. Ned drove, and Dai drowsed, conscious of satisfaction. It was a good life, and he would not change it for any other.

It was almost day. He stumbled wearily up to bed, and discovered Elliott curled comfortably round the hot water bottle that Mollie had put for her father. Dai pushed the cat aside and crawled under the covers. Another day would soon begin. Another surgery. More operations. More calving cows and foaling horses and lambing sheep. Sheila roused herself and spoke sleepily.

'It was a good party,' she said.

She sat up.

'And we heard that we've won the appeal.'

Dai stretched luxuriously and smiled at the rising sun. Elliott turned himself, and curled up more comfortably. The first rays of dawn glittered on the Roman floor that Elliott had discovered. Out on the fells a fox barked, his voice bridging the gulf of centuries.

'It's a good life,' Dai said, but no one heard him. Sheila was asleep.

A SELECTED LIST OF FINE NOVELS
THAT APPEAR IN CORGI

All these books are available at your bookshop or newsagent: or can be ordered direct from the publisher. Just tick the titles you want and fill in the form below.

CORGIBOOKS Sales Department, P.O. Box 11, Falmouth, Cornwall.
Please send cheque or postal order, no currency, and allow 10p to cover the cost of postage and packing in the U.K. (plus 5p each for additional copies).

NAME (Block letters) ....

ADDRESS ....

....

(FEB 75) ....OP3............

While every effort is made to keep prices low, it is sometimes necessary to increase prices at short notice. Corgi reserve the right to show new retail prices on covers which may differ from those previously advertised in the text or elsewhere.